I0673253

Death at the Presidents Church
A Dupree Sisters Mystery

by

Allen B. Boyer

This book is fiction. All characters, events, and organizations portrayed in this novel are the product of the author's imagination or are used fictitiously. Any resemblance to actual persons—living or dead—is entirely coincidental.

Copyright 2016 by Allen B. Boyer

All rights reserved. No parts of this book may be reproduced or transmitted in any form or by any means, electronic or mechanical, including photocopying, recording or by any information storage and retrieval system, without written permission from the author, except for the inclusion of brief quotations in a review.

For information, email **Cozy Cat Press**, cozycatpress@aol.com or visit our website at: www.cozycatpress.com

COZY CAT
P R E S S

ISBN: 978-1-946063-04-5

Printed in the United States of America

Cover design by Paula Ellenberger
www.paulaellenberger.com

1 2 3 4 5 6 7 8 9 10

For Charlotte Bouton, the pride of Cape May

PROLOGUE: SILENCE IN THE CITY

Silence. It is something a metropolitan city like Washington D.C. rarely gets to experience. Between people walking around, taxis running at all hours, and buses bringing tourists in and out of the city, it's rare for any part of the nation's capital to find a second of silence during the day. However, there are times buried deep in the darkness of a late night, when a city block gets to experience a few fleeting moments of peace. On one particular evening in Washington, a street that runs by St. John's Episcopal Church was experiencing just such a moment.

It was well past midnight and the street was filled with a perfect blend of darkness and silence. No people were passing along the sidewalks. No cars were driving down the street. It was calm and quiet in the late night hour. With the White House in the distance, looking luminous in the darkness, it was a tranquil moment for anyone who happened to walk by.

Suddenly, the hush that filled this street was interrupted by two voices. At first the voices spoke softly and their words seeped into the shadows. A few seconds later, the words being exchanged began to grow sharper and angrier. The tone of their conversation became less cordial. Their voices grew louder and began to echo down the city block. Then one voice shouted so loudly it pierced the night in a way that no other sound had done before on this street. A few seconds later, the silence returned and washed away the echo of that deafening scream.

On this street, filled with darkness and calm, one lone figure appeared from the church and ran down the sidewalk. The figure turned a corner and sprinted up a side street without making a sound. Once gone, a sense of stillness returned and another moment of silence began.

Like before, no cars passed by and no voices could be heard. Yet, there was one person lingering along this city block. A person who was not walking, or talking or even appreciating the view of the White House. A person just outside of St. John's Episcopal Church. A person lying on the steps leading into the church. A person who appeared to be still, silent…and lifeless.

CHAPTER ONE: THE VISIT

It appeared to be the most unlikely place to speak of a murder. A narrow red-bricked house nestled along a quiet side street near Lafayette Square, a public park in Washington, D.C. The only things that made the home stand out were the pink blossoms bursting from the flower boxes under the windows. It was a house that appeared too bright and pleasant to host a guest seeking information about a crime. Yet, as he stood on the sidewalk staring at this most charming home, Neil Cabbott knew full well this was the place where he was going to go to speak of a murder.

When he drew closer to the house, he found a wrought iron fence wrapped around the small property. In a metropolitan city like Washington, he thought it was a meager attempt to provide a sense of security for the two elderly inhabitants of the home. The sidewalk led to an iron gate at the center of the fence. He opened the gate and followed the footpath through. The hinges to the gate squeaked when he closed it. He continued along the narrow walkway, which cut through a small yard and led straight to a narrow front porch.

Stepping up to the porch, he took one nervous breath before curling up his fingers and knocking on the front door. He waited for a response, his fingers tapping impatiently on his belt.

Suddenly the door swung open to reveal an old woman standing in the doorway.

She was tall and lean with a white blouse and a navy blue skirt. Her face had a dash of makeup on it to distract from some wrinkles around her cheeks and under her eyes. Her hair had a hint of auburn color to balance out the strands of gray that he noticed. He guessed the auburn came courtesy of her hairdresser. His eyes were also drawn to her red lipstick, which made her smile a bit warmer when she looked at him.

"May I help you?" she asked, adjusting her glasses.

"Are you Mrs. Dupree?" Neil asked.

"Miss Dupree," she corrected and her face melted into a broad smile that revealed perfectly straight white teeth from behind her lips. "Never married."

The expression on her face told him there were no regrets that accompanied the "Miss" title to her name. In fact, her wide grin caused him to offer a slight smile in return.

"My name is Neil Cabbott. We spoke on the phone a few times about...a murder," he said, trying not to let his nervous feelings mash his words together. He ran his fingers through his thick dark hair and pushed it to the side. Miss Dupree remained silent and he smiled again at the tension that he was sensing in this moment.

"So you're the Mr. Cabbott who's been calling our house? The reporter from the *Washington Journal*?" Miss Dupree finally spoke up.

"That would be me," Neil replied, fumbling to show a newspaper ID to back up his claim. "Now when I called on the phone I believe I spoke to both you...and your sister. So which one are you...Ruth or Charlotte?"

"I'm Charlotte," she answered and then she opened the door a bit wider. She waved him in with one hand while she swatted at a fly with the other. "Please come in, Mr. Cabbott. I'm only inviting you inside...not the flies!"

Neil turned and took one quick step through the doorway. Once inside, he heard the door shut behind him. He looked around and found himself standing in a dark narrow hallway with hardwood floors and pale walls extending before him. Up ahead he saw what looked like a kitchen filled with sunlight. He also heard the sound of shoes smacking against the kitchen floor. It was like someone was tap dancing in the kitchen he thought. His focus on the sound was interrupted by a fly that buzzed right in front of his face. Neil half-heartedly swatted at it while he looked back at Charlotte, who shook her head in disapproval of the fly.

"Summer does bring out the bugs," he observed.

"Nature's little nuisance, if you ask me," Charlotte replied and she gestured for him to follow her down the hallway. "Let's move to the sitting room. Of all the rooms in our house, this is the one room that's best illuminated by the morning sun. I think it will be a fine place for us to chat."

"I'll need good lighting to take my notes," Neil commented and he waved a small notepad and pen in the air.

"Well, isn't that refreshing," Charlotte smiled, stopping in the hallway. She pointed at the notepad. "I usually don't see young people like yourself taking notes by hand anymore. Wouldn't you prefer to be poking at a smart phone while we speak?"

"In college I learned the hard way that technology isn't one hundred percent fool proof," Neil replied, fumbling with his notepad. "When I was in my junior year, a virus took out my laptop and I lost everything for my classes. I don't trust saving my stuff to a cloud, either. When I work I always try to write down my notes. Since I'm not in college anymore I don't wanna take chances with losing my job because of a computer virus."

Charlotte smiled at the parts of his explanation she understood. The conversation hit a lull and Neil could sense the awkward silence that was building between them. Then he heard the sound of shoes tapping from the kitchen again. The rhythmic sound echoed through the hallway, causing Neil to become curious about the source of the noise.

"Do you hear that?" he finally asked.

"It's my sister," Charlotte said, her tall lean frame turning to look up the hall.

"Ruth?" he asked.

"Yes, Mr. Cabbott. Let me go see what my little sister is up to," Charlotte said before heading for the kitchen and leaving Neil alone in the hallway.

"Take your time!" he called out.

He lingered in the hallway, tapping his notepad and letting his eyes roll over the details of the setting. The dark wood floors crackled under his shoes. The pale walls wrapped around his view. Halfway down the hall, he spotted a small mahogany table filled with framed pictures. He stepped up to the table and found photos of the sisters.

Some pictures were of the sisters when they were younger, or so he thought. His eyes settled on one black and white photo of a young woman in a dress standing next to a young man in a suit. The longer he looked at the picture the more his curiosity grew. After studying the photo for a good minute, Neil could feel himself quietly laugh at what he'd found.

"My sister will join us in a moment," Charlotte stated, returning to the hallway. "She's busy preparing some tea and biscuits for us. When we have guests, I take care of the conversation while she takes care of the refreshments. That's how we entertain."

"Refreshments really aren't necessary," Neil said with a wave of his hand.

"You know, my sister makes such a fuss over any guest we have here," Charlotte replied, then pointed to down the hallway. "She's better with the social details.

Now follow me, Mr. Cabbott. I'll show you to a comfy couch to sit on."

"Before we go…may I ask about this one picture?" Neil said and he waved his pen at the black and white photograph that he found so interesting. Charlotte smiled and stepped over to the small table. Neil gestured to the young woman who bore a striking resemblance to Charlotte. He also pointed to the person standing next to her. He was a handsome young man who was easily recognizable.

"Is that you with…John Kennedy?" Neil finally asked.

"Why, yes, it is." Charlotte smiled and then she gave one quick nod to the photo. "We were quite young back in those days. I was right out of high school, working as a secretary for a representative. Kennedy was a representative for his district in Massachusetts. The office I worked in was right across the hall from him. I remember one day when Senator Kennedy came in complaining of a splitting headache. Nobody on his staff had an aspirin. I dug in my purse and found one. When I handed him the aspirin…it summoned that famous Kennedy smile. A short while later, he returned to my office, feeling much better. Before I knew it he threw his arm around me and said he needed a picture of the angel who'd saved him from that headache. Ever since that day, he always called me his "Aspirin Angel." If he didn't have an aspirin in his office, he'd always come across the hall looking for me."

"So you saw him more than once?" Neil asked.

"When you work for a representative in the House, I'm sorry to say that headaches become quite common," Charlotte sighed. "Late nights and tight schedules made for stressful days. That's why I always kept a big bottle of aspirin in my office for my boss and for Kennedy."

"Well…that's a good story," Neil laughed.

"Maybe you'd like to write an article about that?" Charlotte suggested while she grinned at the picture. She turned to him and the grin faded. "It's a good story…but I know it's not the kind of story you came to hear, is it Mr. Cabbott?"

"You're right," Neil quietly replied, tapping his notepad against his hand.

"Sister!" a woman's voice echoed down the hallway. "I'm in the sitting room. Please bring our guest in here!"

"I think Ruth is ready for us," Charlotte stated in a very casual way. Neil followed her through the hallway and into a formal sitting room complete with two full-length windows, fluffy white chairs and a matching couch long enough for four people to sit comfortably.

He stepped onto a large beige throw rug that filled the center of the room. Seated in one chair was a much shorter woman than Charlotte. Her hair was white, short and swept to the side. Her glasses made her blue eyes appear bigger and she had a nose that was more than well suited to keep her glasses from sliding down.

"Hello. My name is Ruth Dupree," the woman announced. She gestured for Neil to come in and he quickly sat on the couch across from her. "It's always nice to receive a visitor, Mr. Cabbott."

"Well, it's nice of you to invite me," Neil replied. He looked at both ladies. "You two have a lovely home. Now which one of you is the older one?"

"Ruth is my little sister by two years," Charlotte stated while sitting down in a chair.

"I see." Neil nodded as he settled into the soft white couch. "Well, you both have a lovely house. In fact, I can even see Lafayette Square Park from that window. I can only imagine how hard it was for you two to buy this home."

"It wasn't hard." Ruth beamed from her chair. "Truth be told, this was our parents' house. This is where we were born and raised. It's very close to our hearts. Right, sister?"

"Without question," Charlotte replied, crossing one leg over the other. "We've had many offers to purchase our home over they years, but we always turn them down. You see, I think when you live in one place as long as we have, it takes on a persona. A presence. It's like a member of the family that is still watching over us."

"It provides us with a nice sense of security," Ruth added.

Neil watched Ruth pour something hot into three white porcelain tea cups, then pass one cup to Neil and the other to Charlotte. He was not a fan of hot tea, but he would try to drink some to appease his hosts. Together the three of them alternated between blowing then sipping from their cups.

While they sipped, Neil began to wonder when he should broach the subject of his visit. Charlotte and Ruth simply stared at him and occasionally smiled at their guest. Sitting on the couch, looking back at them, Neil felt like they were waiting for him to entertain them with some sort of story or a song. While he pondered what to do, a blur of fur appeared from the corner of his eye and hopped up on the couch beside him. His head snapped to the side before realizing what was sitting next to him.

"Hello there…cat," Neil said, shifting in his seat a bit.

"Her name is Mezzo," Charlotte said. "She won't hurt you."

"It's okay, I like cats," Neil said and he reached out and managed to give the cat one pet down the back. His nature as a reporter began to form questions about the cat's most unusual name. "Why Mezzo?"

"As in mezzo soprano," Ruth stated and she glanced over to Charlotte.

"Why would you name your cat after an opera singer?" Neil asked.

"We're opera fans," Charlotte added.

"Get on her bad side and you'll find out," Ruth giggled.

"Yes," Charlotte agreed. "Like any good mezzo soprano, she's got a good voice and she's not afraid to use it."

"I see." Neil nodded and he cast an uncertain smile to the cat.

"So we've read some of your articles," Charlotte began. "You have a nice style of writing, Mr. Cabbott. We think the *Washington Journal* has one fine reporter in their midst."

"Thank you," he replied, his smile growing wider and more genuine after hearing such an unexpected compliment. "As a writer, I don't get to talk to readers all that much so what you said means a lot to me."

"How long have you been with the paper?" Ruth asked, before passing a small tray of biscuits to him.

"Six months," Neil softly replied, taking a biscuit off the tray before passing it to Charlotte. He took a bite of the biscuit and began to reflect on his statement. "Well…five months and two weeks would be more accurate."

"I see." Charlotte nodded.

"I think what you do is a noble profession," Ruth observed. "You know, President John Adams once said, "A pen is certainly an excellent instrument to fix a man's attention and to inflame his ambition." I think that's what good writers like you do for newspapers,

Mr. Cabbott. I think you give us something to focus on and think about when you write an article."

She noticed how the words caused her guest to grow red in his cheeks just a bit before mustering up some reply to her compliment.

"Well…thank you for saying that," he mumbled and then he tapped his pen on his notepad, cleared his throat and sat up a little straighter. "So…the reason I asked to meet with you is because I was hoping you could answer some questions for me."

"What kind of questions?" Charlotte asked, feeling her back grow straighter.

"It's about that murder," Neil answered.

He paused for a moment, but was surprised to see that the four words that just left his lips didn't seem to diminish the perky expressions on the faces of his hosts.

"Oh, that," Ruth giggled before finishing her biscuit.

"You see, when they first hired me at the *Journal*, they had me writing up obituaries," he explained. "Now sometimes a family will write one for their deceased…but a lot of people don't have that benefit. So for the first few months I worked for the *Washington Journal* I wrote lots of obituaries. I guess they liked what I wrote because after a few weeks they changed my assignments to writing up police reports"

"That sounds more exciting," Ruth stated.

"Always good to get a promotion," Charlotte chimed in.

"It was a good change," Neil replied and he nodded to both sisters. "During my first week of monitoring police reports, I noticed some irregularities between one particular obituary I wrote and the police report I saw about it. It was a police report for the death of a homeless man.

I had written an obituary for that homeless man one week earlier. Once I saw the police report and compared the two I began to notice some…irregularities."

"Irregularities?" Charlotte asked.

"Inconsistent birth dates," Neil explained with a bit more confidence in his voice. "At first when I checked the police report about the death with the information I'd been given for the obituary, I found that the birth dates didn't match."

"Facts are stubborn things," Ruth grinned. "You know, President Reagan said that and he was right, in my opinion."

"Ruth quotes presidents to me all the time," Charlotte sighed and she rolled her eyes. "Some days, a few too many times, if you ask me."

"I'm sorry…but it did seem an appropriate quote to use," Ruth sighed.

"Anyway," Neil continued, "that mistake caught my eye,"

"But people make mistakes all the time, Mr. Cabbott," Charlotte observed. "Perhaps that's all it was. Just a simple error."

"You're right," he said. "One mistake is understandable…but there were others."

"More than one?" Charlotte asked.

"Along with the birthdate, they listed the name incorrectly by using the middle name instead of the last name of the person who'd died," Neil recalled. "So between the name and the birthdate, I just decided to make some phone calls to get the facts straight before I wrote my article."

"And did you get to the truth?" Charlotte asked.

"No," Neil quickly responded.

His answer caused Charlotte and Ruth to turn and look at each other. Charlotte leaned forward a bit and Ruth rubbed her chin with her index finger.

"That never happens to us," Ruth said. "We always know who to talk to if we need to get to the bottom of something, don't we sister?"

"No one likes a bragger, Ruth," Charlotte scolded. "Please continue, Mr. Cabbott."

"Neil," he replied. "Please, call me Neil."

"Very well, Neil," Charlotte nodded. "Tell us more about these…inconsistencies."

"Well, it didn't help that the police were giving me the runaround," Neil continued. "I told my editor what was happening, but he told me to move on and forget about the story. He said a story about a homeless man's death didn't have any legs or sell papers. Now I know I was in college just last year, but I have to believe I'm onto something big when the police *and* my editor are both trying to shut me down. I wanted to tell my editor that what he was doing was crap…but I didn't want to get fired. That's when my editor suggested I call you two for help. He said you two knew Washington better than me and that it would help me with this story. All I want are the facts, ladies. Can you help me?"

"It sounds like you're a young man of principle looking for the truth," Charlotte grinned. "How refreshing in this town."

"Thomas Jefferson once said, "In matters of principle, stand like a rock," and I believe that's what you're doing, Mr. Cabbott," Ruth observed.

"Yes," Charlotte said before shaking her head at yet another presidential quote. "I agree with my sister. We applaud you for that, Neil. To be young and idealistic is a wonderful combination."

"I wish my editor thought so," he sighed. "I'm beginning to think he sees me as a pest."

"And who is your editor?" Ruth asked.

"Daniel Buchanan," he replied.

"Oh my goodness," Charlotte grinned and she glanced at her sister. "We played cards with Danny's mother for many years before she died. He has to be coming up on retirement soon. He was always such a bright young man."

"I saw him not too long ago," Ruth mumbled. "He's getting some gray hair which, in my opinion, doesn't suit him."

"Well, he seemed to think you two could, in his words, 'give some insight' into helping me find out what I needed to know," Neil said before tapping his notepad on his knee. "I find Washington to be such a confusing town. It seems like every person I talk to about this story tries to shut me down when I ask questions. I'm not from around here and maybe I'm just too direct with people. I moved here from Iowa. Are people in Washington all that different?"

For the first time since setting foot in their home, the sisters grew silent. Both Charlotte and Ruth began to sip their tea, which had cooled somewhat. Neil was not a tea fan, but he kept the cup in his hands out of respect for his hosts.

"I'm sorry, Charlotte, but this will be my last quote for the day," Ruth said.

"Not another one," Charlotte mumbled while she drank her tea.

"John Kennedy used to say that Washington is a community of Southern efficiency and Northern charm," Ruth observed.

"What does that mean?" Neil asked.

"It means that this town can be quite confusing to even the smartest people who come here to live," Charlotte said.

"So how long have you lived in Washington?" Ruth asked.

"Five months and two weeks," Neil replied.

"And you said you moved here from Iowa?" Ruth asked before drinking more of her tea.

"That's right," he said and for the first time Neil felt comfortable enough to put his teacup down. "It's not like I just stepped out of a cornfield when I moved here. Before I came here, I Googled Washington, D.C. and learned as much as I could about the city. I did a lot of research with Google. You know, Google was very helpful. I learned a lot."

"Google?" Ruth asked, her eyebrows lowering. "Is that the first name or the last name of one of your friends?"

"Sounds like a dog's name to me," Charlotte laughed.

"It's not a person," Neil smiled. "It's a website. You know...the Internet?"

"We really don't bother with technology," Charlotte said.

"I know a lot of young people at our church who think they're quite smart because of their smart phones," Ruth observed. "Take away those phones and they'd be pretty dim, if you ask me."

"That's an interesting observation," Neil grinned.

"I must agree with my sister," Charlotte pointed out. "There are limits to what you can learn from a computer screen. It's one thing to look up facts, but it's quite another to know the context in which those facts fit together. Now if you'd ask your smart phone about our nation's capital, I'd suppose you can learn about a nice restaurant or a few names of streets. However, there are things about Washington that you have to experience to give those facts some depth. My sister and I know things about the people in this town that go back generations. We've looked this town in the eye, know its stories and know the people who've lived here. Your friend, Google, might know facts...but it doesn't know how those facts fit into this city."

"So what can you tell me about Washington?" Neil asked. "What should I know?"

"Where to begin," Charlotte sighed and she looked over at Ruth and shook her head.

"My sister and I are products of Washington Society, Neil. Our mother was part of the society that welcomed Franklin Roosevelt and all of his polished charm to Washington. Then our mother struggled to overlook what she called the "Midwestern manners" of Harry and Bess Truman."

"Did you know them?" Neil asked, opening up his notepad and pulling out his pen.

"Our mother did," Ruth nodded.

"That's another story for another time," Charlotte stated. "The point I'm trying to make is that when you're raised in social circles like we were, you realize that the more people you know, the more you understand what really goes on in this town. It's the kind of insight that some people who are new to Washington never learn."

"We've been here for more than seventy years," Ruth pointed out. "We've made lots of friends in this town. Over the years those friends have kept us informed on everything that happens to certain families and certain people of power in Washington. High society isn't just a frivolous dessert to indulge in from time to time. It's right up there with the meat and potatoes."

"All this is to say that the death of a homeless man was something that never caught our eye," Charlotte stated. "Then one morning...when I read your article over breakfast...that set my wheels in motion."

"My article did that?" he asked.

"I almost didn't read it," Charlotte recalled. "It's sad but many homeless people die in Washington every year. It's barely a story to me anymore."

"What you wrote motivated us to ask questions and find out more about this unfortunate death. For you see…my sister and I knew the young man who died."

"The homeless man?" Neil asked.

"He wasn't all that homeless," Charlotte said. "He actually came from a rather large home and a very influential family here in Washington."

"Tell me more," Neil asked, and he sat back on the couch.

He glanced over to the almond colored cat beside him, which was now stretched out and licking its front paw. It seemed to Neil that everyone in the room was growing comfortable with him. He opened his notepad, clicked the top of his pen, and then nodded to Charlotte to begin to tell him a long story about the death of a homeless man.

CHAPTER TWO: COFFEE, TEA, AND A MYSTERY

This story begins on a memorable Sunday morning in April. Ruth and I were attending our church, St. John's Episcopal Church, which is located near Lafayette Square. It's a small church that we used to walk to as children with our parents and still attend every week. On this particular morning we saw the same faces in the congregation and went through the same routines of worship like any other Sunday. However, there was something in our church that made this morning more unusual than others. Perhaps that's why it still lingers in my mind.

For the first time since the presidential elections, the newly elected President of the United States and his wife were in attendance. While it was a nice surprise, it is not all that uncommon. Since St. John's is the closest church to the White House, it has been a tradition that sitting presidents visit our church. In fact, every president going back to James Madison has been to our church at least once.

So on this particular morning, we could see the president and First Lady clear as the sky, sitting in a pew two rows up from where my sister and I were seated. From our pew, I had a clear view of the back of the new young president's head. Dressed in a navy blue suit, his dark curly hair and broad shoulders were fixed directly in my line of vision. I quickly concluded that this young president appeared to have perfect posture.

Throughout the service, I noticed other details. How engaged the president was with the sermon and the scripture readings. How he looked down to sing at the right times. How he looked up for the sermon and the scripture readings and how he didn't even whisper to his wife one time. I also kept one eye on the First Lady to see how hints of her lavender dress could be spied just above the church pew she was sitting in. Looking around at my fellow parishioners, I could tell the younger members were abuzz with excitement over the presence of this couple. Yet, I did not share their enthusiasm. I couldn't get swept up in the excitement that filled the air. This was a scene that Ruth and I were accustomed to seeing.

Having attended St. John's Church all of our lives, we've seen our share of presidents in our church. We first started coming to the church with our parents when we were little girls. Ruth and I even sit in the same pew that we did with our parents. Over the years we've grown quite accustomed to seeing Presidents and their wives visit our church from time to time. Perhaps that's why some people refer to our church as, "The Presidents Church."

Thinking back, I can remember seeing many Presidents and First Ladies. I can recall Mamie Eisenhower in our church looking quite pleasant in a pink dress. She always wore a pearl necklace with matching earrings, which I quite liked as a young girl. While Mamie had good fashion sense, I can also recall how Jackie Kennedy was all style. Like President Kennedy, she was young and fit and whatever clothes she wore complimented her perfectly youthful frame.

There were also a few Sunday mornings when I remember seeing President Reagan and his wife visit. As a young woman, I remember how Mrs. Reagan always wore red dresses that looked like they were sewn from the best flowers in her Rose Garden. I can also remember seeing the Clintons visit, and thinking how Mrs. Clinton was less formal, preferring pants suits over dresses.

When I reflect on my life, I've seen many Presidents and First Ladies visit my church.

While it was nice to see them, the presence of our new President and First Lady simply didn't interest me on this particular morning. What I found more interesting than the visitors from the White House sat in a pew that was across the aisle from the First Couple.

To the left of us was a set of pews where I saw a family sitting together. It was a family that I hadn't seen in St. John's Church for a number of years. I knew the parents well and over the years my sister and I had enjoyed watching their children grow into adulthood. As was so often the case when children grow up, they go off and start their own lives and leave the parents to come to church alone. For the longest time, the parents came to church by themselves. Now here they all were, gathered together on a day that was not a holiday, not a special day on the church calendar, not a day that was significant in any particular way.

I let my eyes slowly move down their pew. The parents, now white haired, sat together with their three grown-up children on either side of them. From what I could tell from my vantage point, they sat quietly together with dour looks on their faces. They sat and, like me, looked none too interested in the President's attendance. After an inspirational sermon, a few hymns, and the collection plate making it around, church was over. I saw the parents and children slip out while the music was still playing. There were no smiles, no eye contact, and no attempt of any kind to exchange pleasantries with the people around them. The family simply stood up and stepped out a side door clearly labeled for emergency exits.

As the music drew to a close, and the service concluded, most everyone remained seated while the First Lady and the President stepped out of their pew and walked down the center aisle. The President offered a campaign trail smile and even shook a few hands. The First Lady was more reserved, offering a slight smile to some parishioners while her husband shook more hands.

While all heads turned to the center aisle to watch the President and First Lady leave, my eyes were drawn towards the side of the church. My eyes were drawn to the family I had been spying on. I watched them all escape out the side door without talking or looking at anyone.

Again, I pondered the significance of seeing the Campbell family together again and the way they chose to leave.

"Why were they here?" I softly asked myself.

It wasn't Christmas. It wasn't Easter. It was just another Sunday. Yet, there was some force that brought Miles and Natalie Campbell's family back to them for the first time in years. I wanted to know why.

CHAPTER THREE: A GOOD BREAKFAST SPOILED

A week went by and I couldn't get my mind off the Campbells appearance at church. Ruth and I had a busy week and there were many things to distract me from thinking about it. On Monday we had some friends over for tea while we discussed some juicy gossip. Wednesday evening, Ruth and I attended a ballet at the Kennedy Center. We even met some friends to play bridge on Thursday afternoon. All in all, it was a delightful week.

Yet, despite all of our activities, I couldn't stop thinking about the Campbells being back together again. While I wouldn't call it an obsession, I was simply curious, and a little nosey, in wanting to know more. The thought became more prominent when another Sunday rolled around. While I didn't mention it to Ruth, I was curious to see if they'd all be back in church again.

After we got dressed, Ruth and I came downstairs and began our morning routines. I prepared some oatmeal and a pot of coffee, while Ruth retrieved the morning paper from the front porch. We met in our small kitchen nook where natural daylight poured in through the windows. We sat down at our small kitchen table, in our usual seats, sharing the paper and enjoying breakfast. It is a most delightful way to start the day, in my opinion. Sharing thoughts on the world with my sister just gets my brain going for the day.

So there we were, eating breakfast and sharing comments on the news. In between articles and sips of coffee, my eyes would glance out the window to the small private courtyard in the back of our house. At this time of the year, the sight of green grass and small flowers tends to make me smile. Ruth calls our backyard a "little green piece of heaven."

We usually devote an hour each morning to the news stories of the day. On Sunday mornings, the paper is bigger which affords us more time to linger over breakfast. Occasionally we exchange thoughts on a headline while enjoying our food. It is always a delightful way for sisters to start a Sunday before heading off to church. However, one morning I found a particular story that caught my eye. I continued to sip coffee and occasionally glance out to the courtyard while I read a few words here and a few words there. Then I came across one fact that caused me to stop eating. The words I read made me focus a little longer before the story simply turned my stomach.

I began to study the article more than once, hoping that the order of the words were somehow incorrect. I hoped that the reporting of this story was inaccurate in some way. I even harbored the wish that I had somehow misread the facts. So there I sat, with my coffee growing cool, quietly reviewing the article over and over before forcing myself to eat the rest of my oatmeal. I absorbed every word and soon came to the sad realization that what I read the first time was indeed true.

"Did you read that piece about Senator Dawson announcing his desire to mount another campaign for president?" Ruth asked. "Now he just lost an election and he has the nerve to say he wants to run again? What do you think about that, sister?"

I barely heard Ruth ask for my opinion on the matter, despite the fact she was sitting right across from me.

"He's...nice," I mumbled, my mind still trying to absorb the article I just read.

"Sister," Ruth replied, her voice growing louder. "Before the elections you were calling him a lightweight. Now you're calling him...nice?"

"Lightweight," I mumbled in a soft voice, not really putting much thought into my reply.

"Charlotte?" Ruth said to me and she dipped her section of the newspaper down to get a better look at me. "You're not listening to me. Are you feeling okay? Are you having a stroke?"

"I'm quite fine, Ruth," I answered and I finally folded up my section of the paper and handed it over. "Yes, Senator Dawson is a nice person but he's also a bit of a lightweight as a politician. He has no teeth for the fight and has no business in the White House. Now, let me have another piece of the paper."

"Take this one," Ruth said, handing me another portion of the newspaper. "There are some coupons in this section you might want to look at. See if we can use them."

Ruth knows I'm the penny pincher in the house. Despite the fact we were given a sizeable inheritance from our parents, along with our pensions, I still feel the need to clip coupons I know we could use.

"Do you remember when mother would complain about Bess Truman clipping coupons in the White House?" Ruth grinned. "Mother was so outraged that someone of such stature would still resort to saving a nickel here or there by digging through newspapers for coupons. I wonder what she'd think of us."

"We only do it on Sundays," I replied, weakly trying to defend my position in case my mother's spirit was eavesdropping from the great beyond.

"I know," Ruth smiled. "I just wonder if mother would approve."

"I doubt it," I said before sipping the last of my coffee. "We both know she had high standards for us. However, if she knew the price for a gallon of milk these days she'd probably be more understanding of the habit."

As I finished my breakfast, I kept one eye on Ruth. Her dish and coffee mug were empty and she casually began to flip through the section of the paper I'd handed her. I kept watching her, waiting for her to find the one story that had turned my stomach into knots. After a few minutes, I was growing impatient for her to locate the article.

"You might want to read the story on page twenty-one," I finally spoke up, waving a finger across the table at her. "There's an item about a homeless man who was murdered."

My words brought silence from the other side of the table, which was usually a sign of indifference on the part of my sister. A few minutes later, I was surprised to see Ruth turn to the page I'd suggested, stop and adjust her glasses.

"This?" she asked, pointing at the article. She shot a puzzled look across the table at me.

"Why would I care about a homeless man?"

"Just read it, sister," I urged.

Ruth grew silent for a minute, carefully reading every detail. Soon she slowly lowered the paper and looked at me with an expression that only a sister would recognize as confusion.

"A homeless man dies of an apparent drug overdose?" Ruth began, her eyebrows going up. "I see it happened near our church. Is that why you wanted me to read this, Charlotte?"

"The name," I said and I waved my hand like I was gesturing for her to keep going. "Did you read the name of the man who died?"

"Let me see," Ruth mumbled, adjusting her bifocals and holding the paper at an angle to get a better view of the words. "Police identified the victim as Joseph Campbell. No other details were given."

Ruth looked at me, still uncertain of the significance to the story. Now between the two of us, my memory of things has always been a little clearer than my sister's. When Ruth would forget something, she'd always defer to my memory for reference. This was one of those times.

"Think back to our church," I started to say before standing up and taking my dirty dishes to the sink. "Many years ago, there was a young boy with beautiful blonde hair and the brightest blue eyes you'd ever want to see. Remember how he always wore a navy blue suit and a matching tie? He came to St. John's Church every Sunday. He was such a handsome little boy."

"I think I remember him," Ruth nodded. "What did we call him…Little Jo-Jo?"

"Yes," I nodded, then I picked up Ruth's plate and coffee cup to take to the sink. I lingered beside her, my eyes dropping down to the horrible words printed on that paper that Ruth was holding. "His name was Joseph Campbell. He would be about the same age as this homeless man that died. I wouldn't have thought of little Jo-Jo but when the article referenced his name, his age and the fact that he died at our church, well that sparked a memory for me."

"You think it's *that* Joseph Campbell?" she asked, her voice growing louder.

"I do," I nodded.

"Oh my." Ruth sighed and her hand covered her mouth in complete shock. "I do hope you're wrong, sister. Little Jo-Jo was just the sweetest boy. To have his life end that way...you know... in the streets as a homeless person....it's such a sad way to leave this world."

"I agree," I quietly answered before cleaning off our dishes in the sink. "I saw his family gathered in our church last Sunday, but I didn't know why. They even slipped out unnoticed and didn't say a word to anyone. This...explains a lot."

"Well," Ruth began, "if he was having problems, little Jo-Jo should have come to us. He could have lived here. We had room."

"Sister, I believe you're talking about the boy." I nodded while I rinsed our dishes and placed them in the dishwasher. "You're remembering the boy...not the man he became. We don't know all the factors that led him to the night he died."

"Point well taken." Ruth nodded and she sipped the last of her juice before handing me her glass. "But....what if it was Jo-Jo? I for one would like to know for sure."

"So would I," I answered, taking her empty juice glass and placing it in the sink. "You know how curious I can be about things."

"You've always been more curious than me," Ruth nodded. "I remember Christmas morning when we were children and I was busy opening presents while you quizzed our mother about the validity of a Santa Claus. You were relentless as a young girl. If I recall correctly, you didn't touch a present that morning until mommy and daddy threatened you with a punishment."

"Yes, yes," I laughed. "I can be curious to a fault. I will admit as much."

"I should say so," Ruth said before folding up the paper and placing it on the table.

"Well," I said, tapping the counter with my finger. "I would like to know how something like this was allowed to happen. The last time I heard about Joseph, his parents told me he was safely enrolled in a private college. How could a son from such a wealthy family go from a respected private college in New England to dying on the streets of Washington? There must be more to the story. Who could we talk to about this?"

"Well, it's not the sort of question we could ask at the Governor's Ball this weekend," Ruth pointed out.

"I agree," I nodded. "Asking the governor's wife what she thought of a homeless man's death would not be in good taste. There must be a way we can discreetly learn more about how this man died."

"It says here he died on the front steps leading into our church," Ruth explained. "Perhaps Reverend Simmons would know more about it."

"That would be a good starting point," I stated.

"At the very least, I would think he would make mention of it at church this morning,"

Ruth observed. "As long as he's not boring us with other announcements first."

"Really, sister," I sighed.

"Reverend Simmons tends to go on too long about things," Ruth stated. "You know that as well as I do."

"Well...it is a lovely Sunday morning," I observed, glancing out the kitchen window. "A good morning for a walk. Let's get dressed and go to church, sister. I for one am curious to hear what the good Reverend Simmons has to say."

CHAPTER FOUR: SUNDAY

When we arrived at St. John's Episcopal Church, Ruth and I sat in the same pew that we've used since we were girls sitting with our parents. My mother always preferred this pew because of the beautiful stained glass window next to it. When I look at it now, the image of the sheep still appears as pristine to me as it did sixty years ago. Dad also liked the pew because he could hear the service better since we were closer to the front. It is for those reasons that, many years later, we still sit in the same pew.

On this particular morning, we listened to the announcements that were made, we enjoyed the organ music being played, and we marveled at how well the choir performed *How Great Thou Art*. When Reverend Simmons read the scriptures, a microphone magnified his soft voice. I quite enjoyed his sermon about the challenges of living each day as a Christian. I could tell that my sister was also engaged by this message. A telltale sign when a sermon is not up to Ruth's standards comes when she begins to dig through her purse for mints to suck on. For this sermon, her hands remained folded on her lap.

Soon the collection plate was circulated, hymns were sung, and the service was over. For most people in attendance, they probably saw nothing out of the ordinary about this particular service. For them, it was just another Sunday at St. Johns. Yet, for Ruth and me there was a glaring omission that left us both stone faced. It was a frustration that my sister was quick to express the second the last hymn was sung to conclude the service.

"He didn't mention it!" Ruth hissed as she followed me out of our pew and down the main aisle of the sanctuary. "He should have said something and he didn't! Sometimes I just don't understand that man!"

I didn't really offer any reply to my sister's words. Instead my eyes quickly darted around for any sign of the Campbell clan reappearing in church. As quickly as they had decided to attend last week, the family was discreetly missing from church this week. After reading about the death of Joseph Campbell, I thought that they might need a steady dose of scriptures and sermons to strengthen their faith. It appeared I was wrong.

"A young man dies at the steps of our church. *Our* church! How can that man fail to mention it?" Ruth asked and she shook her head at the omission. "Reverend Simmons didn't even ask the congregation to pray for that man's soul. I mean, my goodness, everyone read about it in the newspaper. He should have addressed the congregation about the matter."

"Maybe he thought everyone already knew about it so he felt no need to bring it up again," I reasoned. "Like you said, sister, it was in the newspaper."

"Well, the issue at hand isn't about delivering bad news." Ruth sighed and her face turned bright red. "The issue is that man's soul, Charlotte. Reverend Simmons should have been asking all of us to pray for that man's peace with God."

"Well," I began, struggling to think of an excuse for the Reverend. "Perhaps it was because drugs were involved. This really isn't the place to talk about the perils of drugs."

"I don't care!" Ruth snapped and her voice grew a little sharper causing some people around us to look in our direction. Mindful of the attention, Ruth took one step closer to me. "He deserves prayers to get to heaven!"

"Lower your voice," I whispered in a way that a big sister tends to do to their little sister.

Ruth knew why I was asking her to speak softer and she looked around at the other parishioners following us out of the church.

"I don't care if he was mixed up in drugs," Ruth continued in a more controlled tone of voice. "We're all sinners. When we die we leave our sins with our bodies and hope our spirit is pure enough for heaven. Prayers do help, Charlotte. Prayers help. I'm terribly disappointed in Reverend Simmons for neglecting that poor man's soul!"

While I had a great deal of respect for my sister's passion on this subject, I was also conscious of some of the looks Ruth was receiving from the people around us. It was how our relationship had always been since we were children.

I was always the child who sat in church, looked at the people sitting around us, noticing little details about them. Ruth, on the other hand, was the one whom my mother said got, "ants in her pants" when she sat in a pew. While I was the child who liked to blend in with other children, Ruth always preferred to stand out. It was a quality that made her quite a handful for my mother. Ruth never cared how her words or actions rippled through a situation. Growing up, mother would often remind Ruth to be aware of how her manners and words affected the people around her. She also reminded Ruth that a good man would never be attracted to an outspoken woman who couldn't control her emotions. It was a piece of advice that my sister and I took to heart. We both embraced who we were as people and never mastered the "control" our mother spoke of. Perhaps that's why neither one of us ever married.

"I want to speak with him!" Ruth demanded, her voice growing sharper. "I'll make my point in front of everyone in this church if I have to!"

"Calm down," I said and I grabbed Ruth by the hand and pulled her into an empty pew.

"What!" she snapped, jerking her arm away from my grip.

"It seems to me that you're more upset with Reverend Simmons than you are about the actual crime," I observed in the calmest tone I could muster.

"Equal parts, Charlotte," Ruth responded. "I'm upset about the crime *and* the negligence of our reverend."

"We will talk to him about this in private," I promised. "Now if you can stay calm, I'd like to quietly leave the church without any more glances from our fellow churchgoers."

"Tomorrow!" Ruth said, and she took a deep breath that appeared to help her regain some composure. "Tomorrow we should ask him about this egregious omission."

Eventually, we made it home. One of the benefits of where we live is that it's a short walk home from church. On this particular day, the walk seemed longer to me because of my sister's litany of complaints. Each block we walked was filled with a detailed monologue about the many problems she's had with Reverend Simmons since he arrived at our church. I knew that eventually Reverend Simmons would have the chance to explain himself to my sister. Having been in that position more than once, I knew the experience would not be a pleasant one for the good reverend.

CHAPTER FIVE: WHO MOURNS THE HOMELESS?

When Monday morning came we were blessed with blue skies and mild temperatures, which is always a gift when spring arrives in Washington. However, the nice weather didn't mellow my sister. Ruth wasn't interested in reading the morning paper and quickly devoured her oatmeal before leading me out the door. Rather than getting a cab, I suggested we take advantage of the nice weather by walking.

With sunshine in our eyes and blue sky over head, we left our house, cut through Lafayette Square and arrived at St. John's Church in a matter of minutes. It seemed strange to be taking this walk on a Monday morning. Weekday traffic around Lafayette Square was a little busier than on a Sunday. While the increase in traffic was hard to ignore, what also caught my eye were the subtle reminders of a new season arriving in our city.

Springtime is that one time of the year when nature becomes a pleasant distraction for people who live and work in Washington. Between the tall buildings, the bustling traffic, and the landmarks that make up the city, one can find hints of bright hues of green starting to grow most everywhere. Whether passing the White House with its meticulous lawns, or simply noticing stray blades of grass in a sidewalk's crack, fresh minty green is a welcome color to see after a long winter of white and gray.

Aside from bright green colors becoming more noticeable, the other pleasant distraction around town is the color pink. That was the color that some trees held since the cherry blossoms were in full bloom. One of my favorite places to walk is down by the Lincoln Memorial where bouquets of bright pink and white trees line the reflecting pool. I was reminded of the cherry blossoms on the Monday that Ruth and I walked to our church.

Just outside the entrance to the church was a tree with full pink blossoms. The sweet smell from the blossoms brought a smile to my face. I looked at Ruth, who was also smiling. We stood for a good minute admiring the color and the aroma drifting down from the tree before walking towards the steps of the church. I took the first step, then paused and pointed down.

"Here," I said and I dangled my finger at the first two steps leading to the main doors. "The article said that they found him here, on the steps, on his back."

"Oh my." Ruth sighed and she shook her head. She stared at that spot for nearly a minute before looking at me. "If it was Jo-Jo, I can still see him as a young boy charging out the front doors of the church with reckless abandon. Do you remember how he'd jump off these steps? He used to say he was Superman flying through the air when he did it."

Ruth grinned at the memory and shook her head again while staring at the steps.

"I remember that too," I nodded. "He would jump off those steps over and over again. He was quite full of life as a child. Such a sweet little boy, too."

"Let's go in," Ruth said and she quickly stepped ahead of me and opened the door. "I want to find Reverend Simmons."

Hardwood floors greeted us when we walked into the worship area in our search for Reverend Simmons.

The dark wood pews stood in stark contrast to the bright white walls and ceiling. At the front of the church, a stained glass window filled our eyes with color. It was a picture of Jesus and his disciples sitting at a table for the Last Supper. Sunlight poured through the window, causing the image of the Last Supper to glow with a heavenly splendor. At the front of the sanctuary, Ruth and I could see Reverend Simmons tending to some flowers that were at the center of the altar.

Reverend Howard Simmons was a middle-aged man, prone to shaving his head as a way of coping with his receding hairline. The most distinguishing features about him were two bushy eyebrows and a slight mustache under his nose. When he spoke, his eyebrows moved up and down like two caterpillars doing a dance. He also spoke with a soft tone, which served him well for having discreet conversations with parishioners. However, that same gentle tone of voice also made it hard for the congregation to listen to him on Sundays. A long sermon, combined with his soft voice, made Reverend Simmons a bit of a challenge for some of the parishioners to stay awake on a Sunday morning.

"Good morning, ladies," Reverend Simmons said, barely above a whisper.

"Good morning, Reverend Simmons," I called out in a voice that I thought permissible for a sanctuary.

Together Ruth and I went down the main aisle. We paused just before the altar where Reverend Simmons gave us a smile and waved both of us up to the pulpit.

"What a pleasant surprise to see my two favorite sisters," Reverend Simmons grinned, tapping his hand on top of the pulpit before stepping down to the main aisle. "So how are the Dupree sisters on this fine spring morning?"

"As well as can be expected," Ruth answered, trying to keep her anger in check.

"As well as God will allow," I quickly added.

"Indeed." Reverend Simmons nodded and he pointed in my direction. "We are all as well as God will permit us to be."

"And what are you doing on this lovely morning?" I began, placing my hand on the pulpit where he was standing. "Working on a sermon?"

"No, no," he answered, shaking his head. "Simply cleaning out some things. Tidying up a little."

"Spring cleaning?" I grinned.

"Something like that." He smiled and his eyes finally focused on us. "So...what can I do for you ladies?"

"We read about that poor soul who died outside the church," Ruth quickly stated and I saw how she clenched her hands in front of her waist and squeezed them in anticipation of the conversation. I knew this was her way of trying to keep her anger in check. "We were wondering why you failed to mention anything about that poor homeless man yesterday."

Reverend Simmons remained silent and I could sense some tension in the seconds that followed from the way he was looking at Ruth. I could practically hear his thoughts, wondering why he was being questioned about this matter.

"Being good Christian women, as I know you are, this is a just concern for you to have," he finally answered and he followed up his reply with a slow understanding nod. "What happened was...quite a shame. I got the call in the middle of the night. Not the best way to wake up I can tell you."

"We read the account in the newspaper," I stated.

"They said the man who died was named Joseph Campbell," Ruth chimed in.

"Yes, that's what the police told me," Reverend Simmons said and he shook his head. "Just some poor homeless person. Of course, I work with agencies that serve the homeless and after a while you see the same faces over and over again. This young man...he just didn't look all that familiar to me."

"I see," Ruth sighed. "As you know, my sister and I are the two oldest members of this church. We've been here for a long time. We suspect this homeless man was part of this church many years ago. Perhaps you haven't been here long enough to realize that."

"Do you know the Campbell family?" I asked and I took a step closer to the pulpit. "They've been members of this church since long before you arrived. Now, of course, the family doesn't come as frequently as they used to. In fact, the children are all grown up and barely come at all. Every once in a while I see them attend a service with their parents. Was it their son who died, Reverend Simmons? Was it *that* Joseph Campbell?"

After revealing our suspicions to Reverend Simmons, I was surprised to see him turn away from us. He appeared to be looking back to the pulpit, perhaps wishing there was something in his sermon to answer this question. He stepped closer to the pulpit and ran his hand across the cover of a large Bible like he was wiping some dust from its surface.

"I'm afraid I can't answer that," Reverend Simmons finally stated.

"You didn't even mention him during the service yesterday," Ruth pointed out and her face grew red, indicating to me that her blood pressure was going up and she wasn't going to hold back anymore. "I would think as a congregation it would be our duty to not just help the living...but the deceased as well. Why wouldn't you ask us to pray for that poor man's soul, Reverend Simmons?"

"The family asked me for a certain amount of discretion in this matter," Reverend Simmons replied and he took a deep breath and slowly let it out. "I...I am simply trying to respect their wishes."

"The Campbell family?" I asked in another attempt at getting to the truth.

"Again, I cannot say," he replied.

"But it's his soul!" Ruth objected, her voice growing sharp enough that it echoed in the sanctuary. "We should all be praying for his soul, Reverend."

"I have prayed for him in private," Reverend Simmons nodded. "If you feel that strongly about it, Miss Dupree, I'd suggest you do the same."

"I have," Ruth quietly replied.

"Well, what can you tell us about the burial?" I asked. "Do you know when he'll be buried? Despite your *discretion*, my sister and I have a pretty good idea of who that man was. We would like to pay our respects to him...and the family."

"I think funeral arrangements are still being finalized," Reverend Simmons replied and he reached over and opened the Bible on his pulpit. "Please don't think I'm being insensitive about this tragedy. It does pain me to see a child of God pass in such a way, ladies. How one goes from being a blessing as a baby to being a homeless man is a sad mystery about this world."

"Yes, it is a tragedy. Perhaps we should have prayed about that too," Ruth said with a hint of sarcasm in her voice.

"Reverend Simmons, the newspaper article I read indicated that drugs were involved," I stated. "Did the police say anything to you about that?"

"Yes." Reverend Simmons nodded and he stepped away from the pulpit. He walked up to Ruth like he was about to convey some big secret. "Between us, I know the newspaper implied that drugs were a cause of death but...I don't think that drugs were responsible for what happened to him. You see, they found clean needles in his pocket, but that wasn't why he died."

"Why would you say that?" Ruth asked.

"Because there was a good bit of blood on the steps," Reverend Simmons answered and his eyes glanced down to his hands and he sighed. "Once the police left, I had to scrub those steps myself for quite a while before the blood finally came off. Nobody would want to come to a church with blood stains near the entrance. I think that's what killed him. Somehow he must have fallen on the steps and split the back of his head open."

"So you think it was an accident?" I asked.

"That's not what I said. I just don't think drugs killed him," Reverend Simmers nodded and he looked at his watch and his eyebrows went up. "Now if you'd excuse me, ladies, I have a young couple waiting for me in my office. I do apologize for leaving you. If I hear anything more about that young man, I'll be certain to call you with some news. And next Sunday, we will pray for the poor man's soul. I promise."

"Thank you, Reverend Simmons," I said, turning to watch him step away from the altar and quickly move down the center aisle of the sanctuary.

"I'll write you a note during the week to remind you of that promise!" Ruth called out, her voice echoing her sentiment.

"As always, thank you for sharing your concern!" he called back before disappearing out the door of the worship area.

Ruth looked at me. I smiled. She shook her head. Together we quietly made our way out of the sanctuary. It was hard to tell if Ruth was satisfied with what Reverend Simmons had said. Together we went into the vestibule before passing out the main entrance of the church.

"Ruth?" I said, following her outside.

"Yes," Ruth quietly answered.

"How long has Reverend Simmons been here?" I asked. "Has he even been at our church for eight years?"

"Seven," Ruth replied, stopping and turning to me. "Reverend Connor retired when I started Social Security."

"Seven years." I sighed and quickly did the math in my head. "That's not long enough."

"What do you mean?" Ruth asked.

"I doubt that he even knows the Campbell family all that well," I said. "Joseph was already finishing high school. He might know them as a family, but he doesn't understand the social status that the Campbells hold in this town. If he did, he'd understand why the family was calling for discretion."

"So do you think he'll tell us when the funeral will be?" Ruth asked.

"When we get home, I'm going to make a few phone calls," I explained. "Whoever this homeless man is, he deserves to be buried properly. I'm curious about who will show up to bury a homeless person."

CHAPTER SIX: HINTS TO A MYSTERY

I gave Reverend Simmons the benefit of the doubt for two days. I held out hope that he might call with funeral news. However, I also knew how influential the Campbells could be, so when I never heard back from the good Reverend, I knew I had to find out for myself. Once I started calling people, I realized that while the news about Joseph Campbell's death was being presented in discreet fashion to the public, the news was not circulating as discreetly in other social circles. There was strong reaction to the news that a well off family could throw out one of their own and let him die on the streets.

After a few conversations, but no facts about the funeral, I made one well placed phone call to someone I knew to be a friend of the family. After a lengthy conversation that involved reminiscing about the old days, I finally got a date and time for the funeral. A few days later, Ruth and I arrived at the right cemetery, on the right morning and prepared to say our goodbyes to our dear little Jo-Jo.

Standing in the cemetery, the clouds overhead reminded me of the occasional bowl of oatmeal I'd have for breakfast—lumpy, gray and unevenly spread. I stood in the cemetery with Ruth and studied the small number of faces that had gathered for this funeral. A cluster of dark coats, dark suits and mournful expressions huddled around one plot.

I took a few steps closer and noticed that the people in attendance were mostly familiar faces. Some of the faces were changed by age yet oddly familiar to me. They were faces drawn from a family that had been one of the most influential in Washington, D.C. back in the 1970s and 80s. Together they stood, young faces and old, gathered together as a family to bury one of their own. The Campbell Clan, as they had once been known in Washington social circles, were out in full force again.

When I think back on the 70s and 80s, Ruth and I would regularly see the Campbells in church. We got to know the parents. We watched the Campbell children grow up. As the years went by, we would try to exchange polite chit-chat with the family after church services. We got to know them quite well and they us. The children were adorable and always wanted some hard candy from Ruth's purse.

When the Campbell children reached college age, and moved on with their lives, the parents started coming to St. John's less frequently. Still, despite the passing years, Ruth and I were still able to recognize their faces at the cemetery. They appeared to be the same faces I'd spied at church a few weeks earlier.

Closest to the burial plot were the parents, Miles and Natalie Campbell. Both had thick white hair, perhaps made more luminous by Miles' dark suit and Natalie's black raincoat.

Together they sat closest to the burial, Natalie's head resting on Miles's shoulder. Behind them stood their three remaining children, all grown and standing with spouses and friends.

The first child I recognized was Grace Campbell, the oldest of the siblings. Grace's dark hair was pulled back into a bun, revealing the one facial feature that I still recognized; the dark sad eyes that always made Grace look older than she really was.

Standing beside Grace was the next oldest of the children, Thomas Campbell. He was tall and lean like a scarecrow, with a reddish brown beard and a long brown ponytail. The longer I looked at him the more I recognized the boy in this tall distinguished looking man. I could still recognize Thomas by his walk and the way he held his hands behind his back while he listened to the minister speak. His head still tilted slightly to the right while he listened, a gesture I could easily recall from when Thomas was just a boy. While he was much older, there were still hints of the boy that I could find in the man.

Ethan Campbell was the youngest. Despite wearing glasses, and standing slightly shorter than Thomas, Ethan's face still looked the same to me. There was a relaxed innocence about how he stared at the burial plot. Standing with his mouth open, his dark eyes flickered with tears. I could easily recall Ethan as a young boy and how he was always a little more sensitive than the other Campbell siblings.

"I'm surprised more people aren't here," Ruth whispered to me.

"I'm not," I quickly answered. "Consider the situation, sister. A wealthy family like this…letting one of their own become homeless. Now that family member is dead. I can understand why they wouldn't want more people here. The shame and sadness must be devastating for them."

"I just don't understand how they could let poor Jo-Jo become homeless," Ruth asked and what I heard was one of the rare instances when my sister's voice was filled with sentiment. "He was such a good boy. I can't imagine Miles and Natalie letting something like this happen to their son."

I could tell that Ruth still had a vivid memory of the boy we both knew still lingering in her heart. While I too had fond memories of little Jo-Jo, there was one distinction that my sister failed to take into account. He didn't die as a boy. He died as a man.

"I think they're here today shedding tears for their son and brother...not the homeless man he became," I said, glancing across the way at the ceremony.

"After the service, let's offer our condolences," Ruth said. "Perhaps someone in the family could tell us more about how all this came about."

"Not the parents," I pointed out. "They must be devastated. Let's not talk to them."

"Agreed," Ruth nodded. "I don't think we should question Ethan either."

"Why?" I asked.

"Don't you remember how Ethan was always the sensitive child in the family," Ruth recalled. "As a young boy, he would cry quite easily. Looking at him today, he's more upset than the rest of the family. I still see a lot of the boy in him."

"That leaves Grace and Thomas," I said.

There was a long pause while we both considered the somber situation. We also took some time to consider whom we would strike up a conversation with after the service was over.

"I'll talk to Grace," I quickly stated.

"Very well." Ruth nodded. "I'll strike up a conversation with Thomas."

With those last words, Ruth and I began to take slow deliberate steps across the cemetery. When we got to a respectful distance, we paused and waited for the family to bury their son and brother. As I waited I watched Reverend Simmons speak with Natalie and Miles with the same soft voice I would expect from him. Then he hugged both parents. I also watched him hug Grace and the other children, too.

In my mind I couldn't help but recall Grace as a child. There was a grown-up way her dark eyes would focus on me when we spoke about school or the holidays. It seemed to me that her words always had a maturity that far outweighed her years. Her thoughts were always older than her age. Of all the Campbell children, Grace was the one that I felt closest to.

So there I stood, waiting for Grace and looking around at the details of the morning. How the cool wind blew. How the trees stirred. How the clouds continued to lumber overhead at a majestic pace. All in all, I thought it was a perfect day to wallow in sadness. A very light rain began to fall. I opened my umbrella and continued to wait. Across the grounds, I saw Ruth pull out a scarf, mindful of the mist, and tie it snuggly around her hair. Together we waited while the service commenced.

Reverend Simmons read a brief scripture and then offered what few recollections he had from meeting Joseph. Next, there was a time for prayer for all in attendance. When the service was completed, the family simply stood by the plot and stared down at the coffin as it was lowered into the ground. I could see the white head of Natalie Campbell shake, which I assumed was from crying. Miles wrapped his arm around her shoulders and held her.

After a few minutes, Natalie and Miles turned away from the plot, arms wrapped around each other, and slowly walked away. The rest of the Campbell family followed their parents from the burial plot, retreating through the cemetery in silence.

"I'm going to go find Tom," Ruth whispered to me.

Right after speaking those words, I saw her quickly set off to track down Thomas Campbell. I turned and let my eyes rest on the sad face of Grace Campbell.

As long as I've known Grace, and that goes back to when she was a little girl, she has always been wise beyond her years. I'll always remember Grace volunteering her time at a soup kitchen in the D.C. area when she was only twelve. I was so proud of her, even though her family did not speak of it in social circles. She also was a talented writer who had her first poem published in a national publication while she was in high school. Grace also was quite good at playing the violin.

All in all, it was a pleasure watching Grace grow up. When she graduated from high school, it was like releasing this bright colorful butterfly and watching it sail off into the world. Once in college, I saw less of her at church. As is often the case with children in a church, when college arrives in a young person's life things are never the same.

"Grace! Grace!" I called out as loud as one is permitted to do at a funeral.

Old age does make it harder for me to raise my voice. I could tell she didn't hear me so I started to make my way across the uneven grounds of the cemetery. The ground was soft and wet, making it a challenge for me to keep my balance while walking in heels. Soon it became clear to me that I wouldn't be able to keep up with Grace's much younger strides.

"Grace!" I called out again, conscious of the other mourners looking at me.

Finally I saw Grace turn in my direction and her feet came to a stop. The closer I got the more I could see that her cheeks were flushed and her eyes were red. When I got close enough to her, I didn't say anything. There was nothing to say. I simply put my arms out and let Grace step into a warm embrace. Together we stood holding each other. After a good minute, it was Grace who pulled back first. She wiped her cheeks and managed a small smile.

"Miss Dupree," Grace sniffed. "Thank you for coming. I...I didn't know you'd be here. It's good to see you. Did...mother ask you to come?"

"Nobody needed to ask me to come," I answered and I offered a smile to help lift some of the feelings of remorse that were clearly weighing on Grace. "I loved Joseph as much as anyone here. That's why Ruth and I are here. We wanted to honor the boy we knew many years ago."

"Thank you," Grace whispered and she pulled out a crumpled ball of tissues from her pocket and dabbed at her eyes.

I remained silent, reached over and rubbed Grace's back the way a mother would to console a distraught child. Grace reached down and took my hand. Together we stood, with a light mist dropping between us. I patiently waited for Grace to take a few deep breaths to collect herself and absorb the morning.

"Such a shame," I began. "Joseph was such a nice young man. How did he ever wind up leading the kind of life he did, Grace?"

"Joey was very strong willed," Grace sniffed. "After school, dad sent him away to college but college just wasn't for Joey. He hated being away from home and he had some terrible roommates. So he and father....just had different ways of seeing things."

"As fathers and sons often do." I nodded.

"Yes," Grace said, and she blew her nose one more time and appeared a bit more composed. "Joey was headstrong about everything. I guess it was just that sometimes he didn't know if his head was leading him down the right path or not."

"Like the path that led him to living on the streets?" I asked, sensing the opportunity to get more information without sounding too desperate to know.

Grace didn't say any more and her dark eyes shifted to her parents. I could sense my words were rubbing too closely to her pain. She began to walk and I followed her to her car. When she opened her car door she turned and looked at me. I gave her one final hug before watching her get in her car.

Soon other Campbell family members also climbed into their respective cars and turned on their engines. Ruth managed to find me and together we stood under our umbrella and watched the line of cars begin to pull away. Leading the line was Miles and Natalie's car. Miles made eye contact with me and in that one exchange I saw no expression on his face. He did not attempt to smile, wave, or show any gesture of appreciation. On a day like this, I could understand Miles' disregard for common courtesy. Yet, there was something about the expression on his face that left me feeling uneasy.

Ruth and I returned to our taxi, which was waiting for us by the cemetery entrance. On the drive home, we discussed the tragedy of a family losing someone so young. I told her what Grace said and Ruth told me about her brief conversation with Thomas. By the time the taxi had reached our house we were able to review the facts from our conversation, but felt no closer to knowing the reason why Joseph wound up away from his family and living on the streets.

CHAPTER SEVEN: LUNCH FOR MR. CABBOTT

Charlotte paused at this point in her recollections. When she thought back to that cool misty morning, a shiver still went down her spine. She looked at her guest and her sister and smiled. Suddenly, the clock on the mantle struck noon. The ringing sound helped Charlotte to pull away from her memories and focus on something completely different. She looked at Neil Cabbott, who was still feverishly scribbling down notes on what she'd been telling him, and then she turned to her sister.

"Ruth," Charlotte began, "do we have anything to offer our guest for lunch?"

"I'm not hungry," Neil mumbled without looking up from his notepad.

"I picked up some sandwiches at the market yesterday." Ruth nodded, practically jumping out of her seat. "I also have some fresh fruit I can serve. Give me a minute and I'll bring everything in. So nice to have a new face here for lunch."

With those final words, Ruth was out of the room and into the kitchen making all kinds of noises with dishes and pans.

"That really isn't necessary," Neil replied, looking up from his notepad. "I'm here for some answers, not lunch."

"It really is no bother." Charlotte smiled. "Besides, entertaining is what makes my sister happy."

"Very well," Neil said, his eyes glancing back down to his notepad.

Charlotte stood up, walked around the sofa once and watched her guest flip through page after page of his notes from her story. After looking at the many pages of notes she finally couldn't remain silent.

"I must apologize, Mr. Cabbott," Charlotte began, pointing to his notepad.

"For what?" he asked.

"All those notes you've been taking," Charlotte said, pointing down at his notepad. "I've been rambling on for nearly two hours about this matter and I'm still not finished. It would be best if we all had something to eat before we continue with this story. At the very least you get to rest your hand a bit."

A few seconds later, Ruth returned to the room with a tray of sandwiches, a bowl of strawberries and some more tea simmering in a fresh tea pot. The activity caused Mezzo to wake from her slumber. She hopped off the couch and snapped her tail once before walking away.

"This really isn't necessary." Neil smiled, putting his notepad and pen to the side.

"Shaking someone's hand when you meet them isn't necessary either, but we do it," Ruth observed. "Sometimes manners make the moment, Mr. Cabbott. Now we have cucumber, tuna, and crab salad sandwiches here."

"That's quite a selection," Neil observed, his eyes lingering over the choices. "Did you make these?"

"Heavens, no." Ruth laughed. "They're the best tea sandwiches you can buy around this part of Washington...or so I've been told by some friends of mine. They recommended a place for me to procure them for your visit."

"Thank you," he said before picking up a small sandwich with cucumber in it. The sandwich was cut in a narrow style and he appeared unsure of whether to use one hand or two for holding it.

"Either hand is fine," Charlotte instructed.

"We're not very formal around the house," Ruth giggled, pulling up the teapot and refilling their cups of tea. "It is a bit early for afternoon tea, but I had everything prepared early this morning so…enjoy!"

She watched him take a bite of his sandwich. The expression on his face told her he was pleasantly surprised by the taste. He looked over at her, held up half of his sandwich and gave her a smile of approval.

"Can you continue with your story while we eat?" Mr. Cabbott asked while chewing his food.

Charlotte nodded and then she sipped some tea. The warm tea soothed her throat, which was becoming slightly sore from the hours of talking she'd done in the morning. She closed her eyes, remembered what detail she'd finished discussing and then resumed her story about the death of Joseph Campbell.

CHAPTER EIGHT: FINDING NATALIE

After the funeral, it was clear to both Ruth and me that we needed to talk to the family some more. It was also apparent to us that we needed a more relaxed setting to ask our questions. As I've learned from many years of gossiping with friends at luncheons, fundraisers, and even parties, the more intimate the setting the greater the trust becomes and the looser the tongues wag.

Weeks went by as we waited for an opportunity to present itself. We continued with our social engagements and while we never crossed paths with any of the Campbell children, we did occasionally see glimpses of the mother from time to time. However, since the funeral, rumors around town indicated that Natalie and Miles were keeping to themselves during their grieving. I had the greatest sympathy for them and respected their privacy. Still, I was hopeful that one day I'd find Natalie at a social event and be presented with a chance to talk to her.

One morning Ruth and I checked our social calendar and noticed there was a luncheon approaching that we were planning to attend. It was also an event that I thought Natalie Campbell would attend. The reason for the event was to celebrate the work of a retiring senator that Natalie, Ruth and I had known quite well.

Senator Danforth Wilson Crawley, the longest serving senator in Washington, D.C., was not seeking another term in office. After representing generations of North Carolinians, Senator Crawley had announced his retirement earlier in the year. What followed after his announcement was a flood of retirement banquets to honor the years of service that Senator Crawley had given to his country. Ruth and I were keeping track of the honors and dinners being thrown for Senator Crawley through the newspapers. After weeks of making phone calls, I was finally able to secure two tickets to attend an event for us to thank the good senator. What Ruth and I appreciated was the sense of civility he brought to a town full of politicians who could be downright nasty.

In the days leading up to the event, we learned that the luncheon was being sponsored by a flower and gardening group that could trace its relationship with Senator Crawley all the way back to the 1960s. I can still recall when Senator Crawley landed in the spotlight with the Lyndon Johnson administration. The good Senator was young and handsome and worked with this group to help ramp up support for Lady Bird Johnson's Highway Beautification Act.

Long after Senator Crawley moved on to other political ambitions, mother still supported this flower club. While she was not a gardener herself, mother did believe that flowers can make the world a happier place. In the 1960s, she passionately believed in Lady Bird's idea to beautify the nation's highways. Long after my mother died, Ruth and I continued to support the group and its efforts to beautify the country through wild flowers and gardening, which was how we were able to secure our tickets. Natalie Campbell also supported the club.

On the morning of the luncheon, Ruth and I found ourselves in The Crystal Room of The Willard, one of the oldest hotels in Washington. White and gold decor filled the room from the carpeted floor to the twenty-foot high ceiling. When we stepped into the hall, my eyes were drawn to the bright white chandeliers. I also heard the sound of voices echoing throughout the spacious room. I saw guests who were dressed in bright pastels to reflect the late spring season. Ruth and I quickly smiled at a group of young women who were chatting and laughing when they walked by us.

"What a perfect place for a luncheon," Ruth observed to me.

"It is." I nodded. "Certainly a good turn out for Senator Crawley."

I took a full scan of the room, spying as many faces as I could. Suddenly, I felt a hand on my shoulder and there was Senator Crawley himself.

"Ruth and Charlotte Dupree," he said with his low tone of voice. "Ya'll made me so happy by coming here today."

Combine that baritone voice with his southern accent and, as most of his constituents already knew, Senator Crawley could be quite charming even before he shook a hand. At least Ruth and I found that to be true from the many times we'd spoken with him.

"Of course we came," I grinned. "We wouldn't have missed it. You've meant a lot to us and our mother. She often said you were that rare combination of a politician and a gentleman."

"You're mama would be so proud of how you supported me over the years," he smiled. "Your parents were my biggest supporters. I couldn't have stayed in Washington this long without them...and you two."

"Nonsense," Ruth said and she waved her hand at him like she was fanning him. "Mother always called you a class act. I think I can speak for Charlotte when I say you've served with dignity and honor...two words we can't use about every politician in this town."

Her words caused the good senator to grin.

"Well," I said, gesturing to the large crowd swirling around the ballroom, "it looks like you have more supporters waiting for you. Don't let us hold you up."

"I know," Senator Crawley said and he gently placed his hand on my shoulder. "I just wanted to thank my loyalist supporters first. So thank you, ladies…and enjoy the lunch."

With those final words, we watched the good senator walk away to engage some more supporters in polite chitchat. I watched him for a few minutes, then my eyes scanned the ballroom at the many faces in attendance. After taking in the scenery, I looked at my sister.

"I don't see Natalie," I whispered to Ruth.

"She'll turn up," Ruth replied and she smiled at the various groups scattered around the room. "Senator Crawley should be very happy with the number of people here today."

"He's a good man." I nodded.

Ruth and I began to walk around the ballroom. With nearly every couple of steps I took I began to see familiar faces in attendance. There was little doubt in my mind that the room was filled with the cream of Washington social circles.

Together we decided to go into the festivities and mingle. In the background I began to hear soft piano music play. Ruth and I walked directly through a maze of bodies and designer clothes that had gathered in the center of the room. We smiled at a few friendly faces and ignored the rest.

"Miss Dupree!" I heard one voice call out.

"Yes," I answered.

"Good to see you here," said a young lady whose face was filled with perfectly applied makeup. The face did not look at all familiar to me but I gave the young lady a nice smile and offered some kind words in reply. I also complimented her on her dress, which led her to tell me about it in great detail. I simply smiled at her words and her enthusiasm.

You see, from a young age, my mother taught us that the most important detail in any social situation is to make the other person the center of your attention. Make them feel special. Whether it's for a few seconds or a few hours, manners and the right words are always key to making someone feel comfortable and trusting of your company.

"Charlotte," Ruth said, "I think we should put our things down at a table. I notice they don't have nametags on the tables, and I want to get a spot closest to the doors to the bathroom. You know how my bladder demands attention when we come to engagements like this."

"Your bladder is a mess," I mumbled.

"I think the farther away we are from the bathroom, the stronger my urge is going to be," Ruth confessed.

"Well, sister, let's go claim a table close to the exit," I replied.

Together we moved across the room, passing numerous members of the Garden Club.

Some faces looked familiar to us. Some faces were young and tended to pass too quickly for me to get a good look at. Some faces were fixed on their phone screens, making it difficult to identify them. Once we were seated, I knew I could scan the room and take a better look at who was present. While many faces filled my view, there was only one face I was looking for.

Ruth led me across the ballroom to the very back corner where a round table was fixed right next to an exit. I tried to keep my eyes on Ruth's back so as not to get separated. I squinted up at the bright chandeliers overhead and smiled at a few friendly faces that made eye contact with me. After weaving our way though the crowd we reached the table that Ruth was quite certain was the closest to the main hallway and the bathrooms. As we settled into our seats, I saw a white haired woman wearing a lavender pantsuit putting her purse down on another table located directly across from us. I quickly recognized the face and stood right up. Not wanting to be left alone, Ruth also stood up and I pointed out what I noticed.

"Over there is Natalie Campbell," I said in a soft voice.

We watched Natalie stroll across the room wearing dark slacks and a white blouse that clung to her trim frame. I often thought that Natalie tried her best to maintain the same slender figure she had as a young mother. However, trying to stay slender at our age simply brings out the bones more than the body's natural curves.

"Get your things, sister," I said, placing my hand on the back of Ruth's waist and gently pushing her forward. "I'm afraid you're not going to get to sit as close to the bathrooms as you'd like, Ruth. We need to go sit with Natalie."

Before Ruth could object, I led her through the ballroom, noting that Natalie was the only one siting at her table. The closer we got, the more I had to remind myself to slow my steps. I didn't want it to look like I was rushing to Natalie. I wanted our meeting to appear more casual than planned. When we were about three feet from where Natalie was seated, I made eye contact with her, smiled, and quickly thought about a light-hearted way to open the conversation.

"I believe your table is for those of us who require a quick bathroom trip," I laughed before stopping right next to Natalie. I gestured to the empty table. "I don't see any of the younger members of the group clamoring to sit here. I'd suppose it's just those of us who find it necessary to cope with a weak bladder. So are you a part of our 'Weak Bladder Club,' Natalie?"

Natalie's face did not change expression. She appeared to be someone who was there physically but mentally still reeling with thoughts and feelings for her dead son.

"I'd suppose I am," Natalie finally replied and she mustered up a brief smile to my playful observation.

"Ruth cannot control herself, can you?" I giggled in another attempt to get this encounter off on the right foot.

"I'm afraid I don't have the bladder I did fifty years ago," Ruth grinned.

"Nothing to be ashamed of," Natalie said, with a wave of her hand. "None of us are twenty-one anymore."

"So true," Ruth laughed.

Ruth and I quickly sat down on either side of Natalie and together the three of us looked around at the younger faces passing by our table.

"Natalie," I began and I took a sip of water before speaking my mind. "I just wanted to express our condolences for what happened to your Joseph. I didn't have the chance to speak to you since the funeral. He was such a beautiful little boy. Ruth and I both remember him so well."

"Thank you," Natalie spoke in the kind of breathless way that the wind does when it gently pours through fresh green leaves on a tree. She looked down at the table and ran her hand over the white linen cloth spread across it.

"Natalie," I began, and I carefully slid my chair a little closer to her. "I was saddened to hear that Joseph was living on the streets. How did something like that ever happen to him?"

Natalie looked up and glared at me for a few seconds. I honestly didn't know what she was going to do next.

"A falling out with his father," Natalie managed to say, her eyes narrowing after the words.

"Oh, your poor husband," Ruth replied and she shook her head with great sympathy. "Having to fight with a son...and then to have this happen....Miles must be so distraught."

"Miles feels no remorse," Natalie quickly answered. She looked at us and her shoulders went up and down in a very subtle manner. "The Campbell men are strong willed, ladies. Both of them were content standing their ground, even if it meant living on the streets for Joseph. I just...can't believe it all spiraled out of control like it did."

"A death in the family is always hard," Ruth said. "I couldn't imagine coping with the loss of a child."

"Children shouldn't pass before their parents," Natalie sighed and she reached up and began to rub her forehead nervously. She slowly shook her head and looked away from the table. "I...I can't talk about this anymore. I'm sorry."

"Of course," I said, sitting back down in my chair "Let's just enjoy lunch and stop talking about it."

"Excuse me," Natalie said, wiping her cheek with the back of her hand before getting up and quickly walking out of the room.

Of course, I felt terrible for making Natalie cry. I looked at Ruth, who was already looking at me. There really wasn't much to say. We didn't get much information from Natalie and we sent her away from our table in tears.

"Well, that didn't go well," Ruth finally observed.

"She probably just needed some tissues and some time to pull herself together," I stated.

"So you think she'll be back?" Ruth asked.

"You know Natalie as well as I do," I said. "She's tough as nails. Once she pulls herself together, she'll be back good as new. She probably won't talk to us anymore…but she'll be okay. I'm certain of it."

A few minutes later, I spotted Natalie Campbell returning to the ballroom where she was greeted by three young ladies carrying glasses of wine. One of the young ladies handed a glass to Natalie. I watched them chat for a few minutes. Quite unexpectedly I watched as Natalie accompanied the young ladies to their table, instead of returning to where Ruth and I were seated. I wondered if it was a clear attempt by Natalie to avoid us. I never knew Natalie to run away from anyone, but in this case I suspected as much.

I watched her sit down at a table with the young ladies who greeted her when she returned to the ballroom. While they were quite animated in their conversations, Natalie participated with the kind of measured smiles one would expect from a person who is known throughout Washington for her social connections. Once all the ladies were seated around her, Natalie pulled out a tissue and began to speak. The ladies adjusted their chairs and directed their eyes in Natalie's direction. After a minute, I saw her look directly at us and gesture with her hand. Like magic, I saw the smiles of nearly every young woman around her turn to scowls when they looked at Ruth and me.

"Oh my," Ruth said.

"What is she doing?" I spoke to no one in particular.

"I think she's made us out to be the bad guys," Ruth groaned.

As the first course was being served, I kept a discreet eye on Natalie. I watched her smile at the attention she was receiving from those around her. It appeared to me that sympathy was the best way for her to hold court over the younger members at her table. It was Natalie at her best, I thought. With so much attention focused on her, I doubted that Ruth and I would have another opportunity to ask her more questions about what had happened to Joseph. From what she'd told us, we really hadn't learned anything new.

When the main course was served, Ruth and I finally realized we were going to be the only ones seated at our table. One lady who had sat with us drifted over to Natalie's table to hear her stories and share in her grief. Every so often, I noticed the eyes of some of the younger ladies glance over to our table. I could tell by the dour expressions on their faces that they were not harboring good feeling about myself nor Ruth. Looking around at the tables closer to us, social connections were being made and once the food was served it was clear to us that seats were not about to be changed.

"Well, sister," Ruth sighed. "It would appear that we are the social lepers at this luncheon."

"Agreed," I nodded. "Knowing how social events work, I believe we're being punished for making Natalie cry."

I followed this theory up with the observation that no one in the room even approached our table to sit with us. Occasionally the waitress would stroll by the table to ask about our food and fill our glasses with water. The busboy also made an appearance to clear dirty dishes. One knows it's a difficult social event when the busboy and the waitress are the only people who make eye contact or talk to you.

"Why do you suppose she did that?" Ruth asked.

"To avoid our questions," I said, taking a sip of water. "Natalie is tough. She's not prone to trusting people with her intimate feelings."

"So you think she did this…to protect her feelings?"

"I have a suspicion that Natalie has not told us everything," I replied. "She has a secret about what happened…which is why she's sitting over there and we're sitting over here."

"Why would you say that she has a secret?" Ruth asked. "She sounded quite sad to me."

"Do you remember when we were younger and President Nixon would come to St. John's church?" I asked.

Ruth nodded before chomping on a fork full of salad.

"I can still recall seeing him in our church," I nodded. "Despite what some people said, I always gave him the benefit of the doubt when he would visit on a Sunday. Then I saw him do something. I saw him do something that taught me a lesson about the nature of people."

"And what was that lesson?' Ruth asked.

"To judge people by what they do and not what they say," I recalled. "You see, after church I remember how President Nixon would always walk down the aisle smiling and making small talk with people in our congregation. Most people in our church found him to be very friendly and nice. I felt that way until I saw him do something that changed my opinion of him."

"Really?" Ruth asked. "What was it, sister? Tell me."

"You see, every time I saw him in church with his dear wife, he'd always do the same thing," I recalled, more focused on the memory than my food. "During the sermon, President Nixon would always hear something the reverend said that Nixon found interesting. During that part of the service I'd always see him lean over to his wife and whisper something. Then he'd always grab a pencil from the pew and write down the thought during the service."

"How terrible," Ruth giggled. "Writing something down in church! The scoundrel!"

"That's not what bothered me," I said.

"Then what was it?" Ruth asked.

"He'd always keep the pencil," I answered, before reaching over and grabbing a dinner roll from a basket at the center of our table. I tore it in two and began to butter both pieces.

"He'd keep it?" Ruth asked.

"He'd tuck it in the vest pocket of his suit coat every time," I replied. "Now even as a young woman, I knew what I saw him doing was wrong. He wasn't in a hurry. He wasn't distracted. He simply took that little pencil and tucked it into his pocket like he owned it. Thanks to Richard Nixon, I learned to judge people not by what they say…but by what they do. He may have been a nice man to talk to, but his actions said otherwise."

"It was *just* a pencil, sister," Ruth sighed, shaking her head.

"That's the difference between us," I smiled. "You always think the best of people, Ruth. I tend to assume the worst. In the case of Richard Nixon, I was right. He turned out to be crooked long after I saw him stealing pencils from our church. Now look at Natalie. An hour ago she was talking to us, very emotional and very much in tears about her son's death. When I look across the ballroom at her sitting with those young girls, she has not stopped smiling. She's laughing more than the ladies around her."

"After she cut us off socially," Ruth mumbled.

"That too," I nodded.

"So what are you saying, Charlotte?" Ruth asked.

"I guess I'm judging Natalie by her actions today…not her words," I replied.

"And what has your judgment told you?" Ruth asked.

"I think she's in mourning," I answered. "She moved away from us because she didn't want us to keep asking her questions. I also think she's simply trying to hide something from us...but I just don't know what it is."

Together we sat quietly at our table, empty chairs around us, and enjoyed a lovely lunch of pan-seared pork, lima beans, and a side of whipped potatoes.

As we ate, a master gardener from Maine stepped to the podium and began to shower Senator Danforth with kind words. The lights were dimmed. Dirty plates were removed from the table and deserts were served. A bright light slipped down from the shadows to illuminate the area around the podium where the speaker was standing. Most of the eyes in the room were focused on the speaker. My eyes were directed towards the dimly-lit face of Natalie Campbell and my mind was filled with ideas on what I'd said that scared her away.

CHAPTER NINE: THE APPLE

Springtime in Washington has a way of romancing my heart. The colors become more vivid. The temperature grows warmer. The season simply dares me to get outside…and I'm someone who never turns down a dare. After being subjected to a brutally cold winter, I always find it easy to get excited when the days grow longer, the sun grows warmer, and there are more outdoor activities to be done. So one morning Ruth suggested we take a walk through Lafayette Square. It was an invitation that merited very little debate.

Lafayette Square is a convenience for Ruth and me, since it is so close to our house. The park was originally considered part of the White House grounds until 1804. That was the year the property was separated and designated as a separate park from the rest of the land that belonged to the White House. In short, it has proven to be a gift to the citizens who live near this part of Washington. This is especially true for Ruth and me.

One of the pleasures of living where we do is being able to take a leisure walk through Lafayette Square. It's seven acres of quiet green grass amongst the hustle of the city. Red-bricked walkways wrap around the grounds, with black metal benches fixed along pathways for anyone who would rather sit than walk. Thomas Jefferson was the president who designated Lafayette Square as a public park. A few years later, the park was officially named in honor of a French officer who helped America secure its freedom in the Revolutionary War.

On one particularly warm spring day, Ruth and I took our stroll around the park. While we walked, my eyes were drawn to the light green buds and small leaves that sprung from tree branches. I also marveled at how the grass looked more emerald than green.

My sister and I smiled at everyone and everything. The paved walking paths around the park were packed with leisure walkers and occasional joggers. The young mothers pushing their strollers. The dogs sniffing and wagging their tails while they pulled their owners behind them. The colorful kites that dotted the sky. The occasional sounds of birds chirping. With so many details to take in, we finally sat down on a bench that had a lovely view of the park and its inhabitants. I took a deep breath and tried to soak in the atmosphere.

"It's such a nice day to be out," I sighed.

"So true," Ruth replied. "I'm sick of reading books, working on puzzles, and watching political shows on TV because it's too cold to go outside. This is the kind of weather I like. No snow. No sleet. Just days like this that dare us to step out and commune with nature and people. Everyone here is smiling and in a good mood. You can sense the possibilities of a new season in the air. Maybe I'll start a garden this year. What do you think, sister?"

"I think spring fills your head with all kinds of ideas," I smiled. "If you want to start a garden, sister, by all means do it. I'll buy the seeds and you can do the dirty work. My arthritis makes it a little hard for me to dig, but I'll do what I can."

My words made Ruth laugh. She was always the one who didn't mind rolling up her sleeves and getting to work on something. I certainly don't mind taking on a project, but I need some time to think and devise a plan before acting. Even something as simple as planting a garden requires me to prepare a plan of action before I pull out a shovel and some seeds. My sister simply likes to jump in with two feet and figure things out as she goes.

"Mother wouldn't have wanted us to dig up her backyard," Ruth sighed.

"Mother kept us in gilded cages," I quickly added. "We were her two adorable birds that she liked to dress up and show off to her society friends. I sometimes believe the only reason she paid for my piano lessons was so she could fix me up, put me out there in front of her tea parties and have me entertain them while they sipped and gossiped."

"Yes," Ruth nodded. "We never did get to play much with the other kids in our neighborhood. We never got to dig in the dirt or roll around in the yard like normal children."

"I'd suppose mother simply wanted the best for us," I sighed. "That's what bothers me about our conversation with Natalie. What kind of mother wouldn't want the best for her son? Why would she really let him live on the streets? Mothers want the best for their children...not the worst."

"She blamed her husband for that decision," Ruth pointed out.

"How long have we known Natalie?" I asked.

"Twenty, thirty years," Ruth answered.

"We've been to her house for many occasions," I continued. "We both know that Natalie runs her house and her family with an iron fist. While he's a good husband, poor Miles is simply the parsley on that family's plate. Natalie is the main course. If she really wanted Joseph to stay at home, she could have done so with one word to her husband. No, there's something more to this story...but we simply don't see it yet."

Ruth nodded and grinned at a small child running by. The little girl squealed with delight and charged down a grassy hill.

"I quite like this detective stuff we've been doing," Ruth said, turning back to look at me. "It's getting harder, though. I feel like we've talked to almost everyone in the family and we still aren't any closer to learning the truth behind Joseph's death."

"Perhaps we're too close to the tree," I mumbled.

"What do you mean by that?" Ruth asked.

"Do you remember the large apple tree that grew on grandmother's estate?" I asked. "She used to try to trick us by saying it was the tree George Washington tried to cut down, but then we would correct her by saying it was a cherry tree President Washington chopped down not an apple tree."

"My goodness, I haven't thought about that in years," Ruth said and she smiled at the memory. "Grandma was always very clever at saying things a certain way to see if we were paying attention."

"Do you recall when we'd go picking apples?" I asked. "The first couple of times, we'd climb up the tree and step out on the limbs to reach the apples. Then grandmother showed us that the easiest way to pick them was to step back from the trunk, step back from the edge of the tree to where the ripe apples were bigger and caused the limbs to bend lower. That's where we always found the best apples. Do you remember that?"

"Yes," Ruth said. "We used to sell those apples for a quarter a piece. We thought we were quite rich back then. What does that have to do with Joseph's death?"

"This is what I think," I began. "I think getting the facts behind what happened to Joseph is becoming so difficult because we're talking to the wrong people. We're talking to the mother, the sister, all kinds of family. I think we're talking to people who are too close to the situation and they're not giving us all the facts we need."

"So who else is there to talk to?" Ruth asked.

"We need to take a step back," I said. "Instead of talking to the family, let's find someone who's a little less emotionally connected with the events surrounding Joseph's demise. Perhaps such a person could give us a different perspective on things."

"Do you have anyone in mind?" Ruth asked.

"In fact I do," I replied. "I think there's someone we both know who could give us insight into this whole situation. In fact, I believe she's the godmother to one of the Campbell children."

"Oh, no." Ruth sighed and she rolled her eyes. "You don't mean who I think you do!"

"I'm afraid so." I smiled.

Ruth rolled her eyes and shook her head.

Sometimes sisters don't need words to communicate ideas to each other. Sometimes we can anticipate what the other one is going to say. However, Ruth and I have taken it a step further. After living together for so many years, we practically know what the other person is thinking before a word escapes our lips. This was one of those times and I could tell my little sister was none too happy with the person I wanted us to visit.

CHAPTER TEN: WEB OF RUMORS

As a child, I was terribly afraid of spiders. Just the way they looked and the way they moved upset me. Whenever I saw one, I'd scream at the top of my lungs. Ruth was always there to come to my rescue, rushing over to smash whatever poor little spider happened to find itself in front of me. Ruth protected me against all things creepy crawly and she still does to this very day.

I had quite a few fears when I was a little girl. Spiders, lightening, even large dogs were just some of the things that would set my heart racing. To help me get over my fears, mother thought it would be a good idea for me to learn about the things that scared me. I can clearly remember one summer when she took me to the library to check out book after book on spiders. I remember one book I read that talked about how a spider can tell when it has captured something by sensing the vibration of the many strands that makes up its web. When a particular strand vibrates, the spider knows where it needs to go and moves quickly to devour whatever it has caught. Such was the case with an acquaintance that Ruth and I knew. Lucille Vance was her name and gossip was her web.

When a rumor got entangled in the web of Washington's most well connected socialite, Lucille, she was always there to quickly devour it.

Lucille is a few years older than Ruth and myself. She's been at the center of Washington's social circles longer than anyone we can think of. Most ladies we know in Washington society strike a balance between social engagements and the responsibilities of family. For Lucille Vance, there was never any balance.

Like us, Lucille never married. While Ruth and I threw ourselves into our church activities and funding good causes, Lucille made the glamor of Washington society her only focus in life. For many years, she lived at the center of luncheons and teas and ingratiated herself to the wealthiest families and the most powerful politicians. She also had an ego the size of the national budget, which she managed to keep in check around the right sort of people.

For as long as I can remember, Lucille had become a pipeline through which gossip flowed to every corner of Washington. There was simply no secret that could resist her charms and her ears. Once in her possession, Lucille wouldn't hesitate to pass along a rumor or secret to anyone she deemed fit to hear it. With her pleasant smile and her quick wit, Lucille always had a way of getting people to trust her and talk to her about the kinds of details one doesn't normally share at social events.

Because of her love for gossip, I knew Lucille would be a good source to discuss the circumstances around Joseph's death. She's always been close to the Campbell family and remembers every detail of their conversations. My decision to go to Lucille's home felt right, up to the moment that Ruth and I found ourselves standing on her door step about to knock on her front door.

"It's not too late to leave," Ruth whispered.

"We're here for some elusive facts," I stated and I quickly knocked on the door. "And let's try not to let her sidetrack us with news about whose husband is running around with what young thing. You know how she can get about sharing her gossip."

"Only pigs enjoy that kind of mud," Ruth mumbled.

When the door opened, we were greeted by Lucille with a pleasant smile and shown to her living room. Lucille gestured to a cream-colored sofa for us to sit on, while she settled her fuller figured-frame into a wood rocking chair with a cushion that resembled the cream color of the couch. I often thought that Lucille's larger body was a refection of a woman who preferred to sit and talk, rather than walk or work. Once Ruth and I were on the sofa, I spotted a bright pink pillow between us with purple stitching that read, "If don't have anything nice to say about someone…sit here with me."

"Don't you two look snug on that couch," Lucille grinned, her round red cheeks pushing up under her glasses. She gestured to a large baby blue upholstered chair to the left of the sofa. "One of you can sit over here…spread out a little bit, ladies."

"We're just abiding by your rule," I smiled, pointing at the pillow. "You know, the one you have embroidered here."

"A rule?" Lucille grinned and she ran her hand over her perfectly styled hair. "I'm afraid that's just for show, ladies. I don't enforce that rule around here."

"Maybe not formally," Ruth mumbled to me.

"What's that?" Lucille asked.

"I just told my sister what a lovely pillow you have," Ruth said in a louder tone and she even managed to muster a less than sincere smile to finish off her comment.

By the look on her face and the way she sat, I could tell Ruth wasn't happy to be in Lucille's house. Lucille tended to be a bit of a show-off with what she knew and that was a quality that put off Ruth. Sometimes Lucille liked to flaunt her knowledge about Washington society to whomever she was talking to. As Ruth pointed out more than once, it was like she wanted to show us she was the smartest person in the room. Unlike Ruth, I could ignore all of Lucille's lesser qualities to learn more about Joseph Campbell.

"Lucille," I began, sitting up a little straighter on the couch. "My sister and I were just at Senator Crawley's retirement luncheon this week and we ran into Natalie Campbell. Such a shame about her son."

"Oh, yes." Lucille nodded. "Yes, Joseph's death will be quite a burden for them."

"I didn't realize he was living on the streets," I said, and I sat back on the couch before grabbing the pillow and placing it on my lap.

"How did that happen?" Ruth asked.

"You know what my father used to say," Lucille began. "He'd say 'Every day presents us with sunshine and shadows. Do you focus on the darkness or do you focus on the light?' I think that's a good way to describe the Campbell family. They had many days in the sunshine, but of late...they've had many dark days to struggle with."

Silence followed this statement and I really wasn't quite sure what to say after such a deep thought from someone I considered to be as shallow as a birdbath.

"Of course, we asked Natalie a few questions about Joseph when we were at the luncheon," Ruth finally said.

"That's right," I agreed. "I could tell she's still grieving, as any mother should be. It just didn't seem like a good time to press her for more information than what she told us."

"That's not what I heard, ladies," Lucille laughed. "I heard you naughty little sisters made her so upset she cried and stormed out of the luncheon. Really, Charlotte, I knew Ruth could be insensitive with other people, but not you."

The news caught both Ruth and me off guard. The luncheon was just yesterday and already Lucille knew about Natalie's emotional scene. I could feel my face get hot and my blood pressure rise.

"You both drew a good amount of attention at that luncheon for what you said to poor Natalie," Lucille grinned. "In fact, from what I hear, Natalie was blaming both of you for taking the spotlight off the good senator."

"*We* ruined the senator's luncheon?" Ruth asked, and I could hear some annoyance in the tone of her voice.

"Such a shame you had to put Natalie on the spot like that," Lucille grinned.

"Lucille," I began, glancing at Ruth with a look that a sister casts to help calm the other. "You know as well as I do that Natalie Campbell is one of the toughest women in this town. From what I could see she was not filled with grief for the entire luncheon. In fact, she was chatting and laughing at a table filled with young ladies who hung on her every word."

"Well, now you know why," Lucille nodded. "When one pays good money for a social event, one does not want to sit with people who are insensitive about the death of a son. At least that's how Natalie Campbell is portraying you both to anyone who will listen to her. How did she phrase it to me? 'They are a couple of sisters who run their mouths without thinking first.'"

Ruth looked at me and all I could do was shake my head at Lucille's words. In fact, I felt like standing up and handing Lucille her pillow. She certainly earned it with those words.

"No matter," I finally spoke and I waved my hand in the air. "Yes, we did speak with Natalie. Yes, she told us that Joseph and Miles had a falling out and Miles had sent his son packing. Everyone knows that Natalie runs that family with an iron fist. Why she simply didn't tell Miles she wanted Joseph back in the house is the question I have."

"And you thought to come to me for an answer?" Lucille grinned.

"Regrettably," Ruth mumbled.

"Let me tell you something," Lucille began, jabbing her finger in the air at us. "Not many people visit me for my charm and wit. Not many people visit for my company. Quite a number of people visit me to have a question answered. You know, ladies, some people put down gossip the way they put down eating candy instead of fruit. Yet, in the end, you hand candy to someone and most times they won't hesitate to pop it in their mouth. You know who loved gossip? President Kennedy!"

"I gave him an aspirin once," I quietly stated.

"Yes, yes," Lucille said and she rolled her eyes like a teenager. "You've told me that delightful story one too many times, Charlotte."

"Oh," I mumbled and my enthusiasm for telling the story quickly waned.

Only Lucille Vance could coordinate a sharp expression, a sour tone and a few words to make me feel embarrassed about one of my favorite memories.

"Now if I were you, Charlotte," Lucille began with a sly grin, "I'd add a few details to that story. Spice it up a little bit. Say that he tried to kiss you, or put his hand on your knee. Anything sordid like that would give you the center of the room the next time you told that story. Everyone knows what kind of a rascal Jack Kennedy was, so taking a few liberties with the facts wouldn't make anyone suspicious. In fact, it might even make you more interesting to listen to, dear Charlotte."

"I think I'm interesting enough, Lucille," I answered, and again I could feel my blood begin to simmer.

"So you say," Lucille sighed, then she paused and made a face like she was disappointed in my response to her suggestion. "Well...back to the matter at hand. You said you wanted to know about Joseph Campbell. You were curious about his...disposition?"

"Yes," Ruth said, leaning forward in her seat. "Since we're here, Lucille, would you mind telling us what you heard that might shed some light on why Joseph was living on the streets?"

"I might have a little light to shed for you," Lucille replied with a hint of pride in her voice. She placed her hands on her lap and laced her fingers together. "But first I want Ruth to ask me in a nice and respectful way. Say 'please' and I'll tell you what I know."

"Why?' Ruth snapped.

"Because I want to know that you're grateful for what I'm about to say," Lucille sweetly explained. "I know your sister values what I'm about to share. I just want to know that you value it too."

Ruth turned to me and her face grew bright red. I could tell she could use her blood pressure medicine. I also knew that the sooner we got what we needed, the sooner we could leave Lucille, which I knew would be a good thing. I smiled and nodded to Ruth.

"Go ahead, sister," I smiled.

"Please," Ruth sighed.

"If you insist." Lucille grinned and she tapped her white hair for good measure. "This happened about a year ago, ladies. Now you know that the Campbells sent young Joseph to the best Ivy League school they could find."

"Yes," I nodded. "And then he moved back home after one year."

"That's right, Charlotte." Lucille nodded. "Do you have any idea why he came home?"

"I assumed it was because of poor academics," I stated.

"Yes," Ruth chimed in. "College isn't for everyone. Personally, I just thought Joseph wasn't a good fit for an Ivy League school. There's a good deal of pressure at some of those schools and, growing up, Joseph never handled pressure all that well."

"Oh, well, let me surprise both of you. College *was* a good fit for Joseph." Lucille smiled. "In fact, he was on the Dean's List for both semesters he was there. You know, he was quick as a whip."

"Well, then, if it wasn't because of his grades…why did he leave?" Ruth pressed.

"This is where it gets interesting," Lucille began, and then she paused to build the tension of the moment. "You must understand, ladies, the Campbell family went to great lengths to keep this quiet…but since dear Joseph is gone, I think it would be okay for me to share this with you. I'm sorry to say that Joseph acquired an addiction to drugs while he was at college."

"Drugs?" I blurted out.

"It was quite sad," Lucille continued. "Devastating for the family to watch him struggle with his…problem."

"Really?" Ruth sighed and she slowly shook her head. "Drugs? Oh, poor Jo-Jo."

"Who?" Lucille asked.

"That was just a nickname we had for Joseph when he was a boy," I quickly explained. "So his taste for drugs came from college. The newspaper article said they found needles on him when he died…but no drugs."

"His addiction…that was the reason he was homeless," Lucille nodded. "Miles took a stand and told Natalie in no uncertain terms that Joseph could not keep drugs in their home. They discreetly tried an addiction center, but even in completing the program there is no guarantee of success. Any type of addiction is hard to break, in my opinion."

"So he sought out help," Ruth said.

"The family enrolled him in the treatment program," Lucille corrected.

"And did it work?" I asked.

"Eventually he relapsed," Lucille sighed, stroking her white hair with one hand. "After that, Miles put his foot down. Natalie, of course, didn't want Joseph to leave but Miles gave Joseph the option of another rehab program. Joseph chose the drugs and the family cut him off, simple as that."

"What a terrible dilemma for Natalie and Miles," Ruth sighed.

"Quite tragic," I nodded. "Knowing someone so young and so smart who has their life cut short by addiction. When you get to be our age, Lucille, you look at a situation like that and realize all the potential lost. That, to me, is the tragedy of it all. He was so smart, who knows what he could have done with his life."

"So, ladies," Lucille said and she gestured with her one hand like she was fanning herself. "Tell me something you know about this situation. You talked to Natalie. Tell me something I don't already know from the newspapers. Something that will keep my interest."

"We know he didn't die from a drug overdose," Ruth announced.

"Really?" Lucille said. "After reading the newspapers, the way the article was written it led the reader to imply that drugs were the main factor in all this."

"He hit the back of his head on the steps to our church," I stated. "At least that's what we learned. Maybe he fell. Maybe something else happened. It really is hard to know for sure. We do know there was a good deal of blood that had to be scrubbed from the steps leading into our church. We just don't know what happened to cause him to hit his head, but we're pretty sure it wasn't a drug overdose. No one knows for sure."

"I see." Lucille nodded and smiled. "There are no secrets in this town, ladies. Some day, someone will speak of what really happened. When they do, I will find out. No one gossips in this town without it passing through my ears."

"If you hear anything, Lucille, please let us know," I said, standing up.

"I will call you if I learn more," Lucille promised and if there was one thing I knew for certain about her, I could trust Lucille to keep her word about sharing gossip.

She was kind enough to walk us to the door, wish us a good day, and renew her promise to get to the truth. Ruth and I didn't have to walk more than a block before we got a taxi to take us home.

All the way home I listened to Ruth complain about Lucille. The hints of sarcasm in the tone of her voice. The facial expressions. The slights in her glances and gestures towards Ruth. Taken as a whole, I could tell it was a much more difficult trip for Ruth to take than me.

While I nodded to every complaint Ruth could muster, I knew deep in my heart that the trip to Lucille's was worth all the stress. I trusted Lucille and knew she would pass along any gossip she heard on this matter. I was also shocked to learn about Joseph's drug problem. Over the years Lucille always took pride in telling us things we didn't know. To do otherwise would go against her nature. It was Lucille's nature I was counting on to contact me when she knew all the facts about Joseph's death.

CHAPTER ELEVEN: BROTHER'S KEEPER

As I mentioned once before, in the history of my church a sitting President of the United States has always come to worship in our chapel. Since our church is the closest to the White House, every president since James Madison has come once or twice while others visited with more regularity. In fact, one of my earliest memories as a child was of Harry Truman and his wife coming to our church on Sundays. I remember all the fuss the first time President Truman arrived at our church. My mother observed more than once how polite he was to remove his hat before stepping into our church. Not all presidents showed that kind of reverence, or so my mother told me. Over the years I've come to see what she meant.

It seems to me that our little church brings out different reactions from different presidents. I've seen some linger in the doorway before taking a few steps into the church to chat with parishioners and shake hands like it was Election Day. I've seen some presidents simply wait until everyone was seated in church before entering and not making eye contact or even cracking a smile. Some presidents have arrived with dour expressions, looking like their chief of staff ordered them to be there. Even during the service, I've seen some presidents act too friendly before receiving a well thought out elbow from their wives. The elbow, I thought, was to remind a president to show reverence for the Lord's house.

The Sunday after Ruth and I met with Lucille, the current president and his wife were back in our church, sitting in the same pew that is always reserved for the president. While it was nice to see, I was more focused on Reverend Simmons. He was delivering a strong admonishment about sin. However, the power of his message was being undercut by the tone of his delicate voice. It was a regular source of concern for Ruth and myself. At our age, Ruth and I are both a little hard of hearing. To have the word of God being muffled by the good reverend's soft voice is a recurring problem for both of us.

While I listened to Reverend Simmons give his sermon about sin, I turned to find Ruth digging through her purse. She looked at me and rolled her eyes from time to time in response to the challenge of listening to the sermon.

"Rolling your eyes is not respectful," I whispered as only a big sister could.

"Neither is making the same point over and over again," Ruth replied before slipping a piece of hard candy into her mouth.

"Finally," Reverend Simmons spoke in a louder voice, "let us pray for the souls of those who live in sin. Let us ask that when these lost souls reach heaven that God can purify their souls and that they can be cleansed of their words and their deeds. Now I'm quite certain that some of you read about the unfortunate death of that homeless man outside of our church. When we pray today, please remember him along with other lost souls so that they may find a home with God."

Ruth turned to me and smiled for the first time since we entered the church. Reverend Simmons had kept his word. More prayers for Joseph's soul were going to help.

Soon the congregation stood to sing the final hymn of the service. While I sang along I allowed my eyes to roam around one more time before settling on a familiar face standing across the aisle from me. When the music ended, I quickly leaned over to Ruth, gently poked my elbow into her ribs, and pointed across the aisle.

'Grace is here," I whispered.

"Really?" Ruth said, putting her hymnal away.

"I want to talk her," I remarked, watching Grace step out into a side aisle and make her way to exit out the same side door her family had used a few weeks earlier. "C'mon. Let's see if we can catch up to her."

"Why?" Ruth asked.

"Because the oldest sibling always knows what her younger siblings are up to," I replied. "We know that Joseph was on the streets with a drug problem. I was just curious to hear what Grace thought about all that."

"Why bother her?" Ruth asked and she followed her question with an expression of sympathy. "Joseph had a drug problem and the family booted him out of the house. What more can we learn by bothering her?"

"As I said before, the oldest sibling always keeps an eye out for the younger siblings," I explained and I smiled at Ruth after speaking. "I've been doing that for you for seventy years, dear sister. You've just been too oblivious to notice it."

"Oh, I notice," Ruth stated as she stepped out to the main aisle. "That's why sometimes I'll say, 'thank you' for your help and other times I'll tell you to quit being nosy and mind your own business. Believe me, sister, I do notice the many ways you try to 'help' me."

"It's a slippery slope being your big sister," I laughed.

"It's slippery for the little sister, too." Ruth smiled.

Together we moved through the long, slow procession of parishioners leaving the church. With each step, I scanned the side of the church, looking for any signs of Grace. Bodies shuffled from side to side, obscuring my view. Then I saw her walk by the exit door, making her way to the vestibule.

When we reached the vestibule I quickly stepped outside the church and scanned the faces gathered around the sidewalk. I saw many familiar faces wrapped in conversation, but no Grace. Then I noticed Ruth wasn't standing beside me anymore. I looked left, then right, then left again before turning back to the church. I stepped back inside the vestibule and spotted Ruth standing next to a rack of candles that parishioners are invited to light in memory of loved ones. Grace was standing in front of the candles.

Wearing a navy blue dress and matching shoes, Grace's dark hair was pulled back into a bun. She looked like one of those perfect models straight out of a magazine. Also, I could see her dark eyes and was struck by how much grief they were carrying in them.

"Grace," I said and I reached out and gently took her hand in mine. "It's so good to see you here this morning. Church is the best place for you right now."

"I live an hour away," Grace explained. "There's a church closer to my home that my husband and I go to but…I just felt drawn here this morning. I feel closer to Joey when I'm here. This church…it just brings back good memories for me."

"You said you have a husband?" Ruth asked and her eyes quickly deferred to Grace's hand where a bright diamond ring caught her eye. "Oh, my goodness, when did that wedding band get on your finger?"

"I got married three years ago." Grace smiled. "We met about five years ago. We have a dog named Marnie that we spoil rotten. My husband and I are very happy."

"Oh, my dear." I smiled and leaned over to get a good look at her ring. "That is such splendid news. Ruth and I never had the good fortune of marrying. You must lead quite a busy life with your dog and your husband."

"Yes…but it's nice having a family to come home to at the end of the day," Grace sighed and she turned around and faced the line of candles arranged on a narrow table. Some of the candles were lit and some were not. Grace reached down, lit one of the candles and smiled. "That one's for Joey."

As I watched her light a candle in her brother's memory, I tried to prioritize all the questions I wanted to ask and not overwhelm her with my curiosity. The expression on Grace's face while she lit the candle told me that the pain was still close to the surface. I watched Grace's hands fold together in front of her waist. Her dark eyes closed and her lips moved in a silent prayer. I looked around and noticed we were the last three people in the vestibule. When her lips stopped moving, her eyes opened and they turned to look at us.

"I know he's at peace now," Grace whispered.

"I spoke to your mother the other day," I quietly began and I stepped a little closer to her before finishing my thought. "She is really having a tough time. Grace, I…I didn't realize that your father had such a bad falling out with Joseph over what I suppose was his drug problems."

Grace looked at me and her eyebrows drifted up. She blinked a few times and her head tilted to one side.

"How did you know that?" Grace asked. "Did mother tell you?"

"I spoke with some friends of the family," I replied and my eyes glanced over at the candle that Grace had lit. "It really sounded like a bad situation for everyone."

"Yes." Grace nodded and she also looked back at the candle. "It was more than 'bad' from what I was told by mom. Joey was a lot like dad...even his temper. I wasn't around to hear them argue, but mother said it was terrible to listen to."

"So what happened to him when he left?" Ruth asked. "Did he just walk the streets day and night? I can't imagine him doing that during the winter. Did he have somewhere to go where he felt safe?"

"There was a shelter that he'd go to sometimes," Grace recalled. "I think it was...a shelter run by Communal Charities. The shelter is a few blocks west of here. Holy Redeemer Shelter I think is the name. When I came home to visit, Joey would meet me here after church. Sometimes I'd walk with him down to that shelter after church."

"Ruth and I are familiar with the place," I told Grace. "Perhaps we'll stop down there on the way home. Maybe we could speak with the man who runs it. I believe his name is Gus."

"How would you know anyone who runs a homeless shelter?" Grace asked.

"Generosity," I said and I offered a warm smile to underscore my answer. "Generosity opens many doors."

CHAPTER TWELVE: A DRY MOUTH

When Charlotte finished this part of her story, she paused long enough for her guest to finish writing. She noticed how Mr. Cabbott's eyes stared down at the small notepad he was scribbling on for most of the morning. When he finished recording her recollections he looked up at her. For the first time since she began to tell her story, Charlotte had grown silent. He looked at her and his head cocked to one side the way a dog would when confused.

"Something wrong?" Charlotte asked.

"I heard of that place," Neil finally said, waving his pen in the air. "Holy Redeemer Shelter. It's not that far from here."

"That's right," Charlotte smiled.

"I got a tip that the police were interviewing the guy who runs that shelter," he stated. "My source told me they were checking into some of the rough characters who've stayed there. Since the deceased had fresh needles on him, but no drugs, it must have gotten the police thinking that maybe his death was a robbery gone bad. They were thinking that the Campbell kid got beaten pretty badly and had his drugs stolen from him. At least that would explain why he had clean needles on him but no drugs to use. Sound theory, if you ask me."

"It's sound…if he ever had drugs on him," Charlotte pointed out.

"Someone doesn't carry clean needles around to be fashionable," Mr. Cabbott shot back. "He was an addict…at least that's what I've been told. There are lots of addicts living on the streets, ladies. I know some cases of regular people who lost their home, their family…everything to get a fix. Given the victim's background, it wouldn't surprise me if he got into a fight with someone over drugs."

"What makes you think he got into a fight?" Ruth asked.

"The police said he had abrasions on his knuckles, consistent with someone who was fighting when he died," he said.

"A fight…" Ruth sighed.

"Can we get you something to drink?" Charlotte asked and she stood up after her question. "I think I'm going to get myself some water. All this talking is leaving my mouth quite dry."

"I'm good," Mr. Cabbott stated, his eyes glancing back down to his notepad.

Charlotte ducked out of the sitting room and into the kitchen. She grabbed a glass from a cupboard, went to the sink, filled it with tap water, and then returned to the room. She took a sip and let the water roll around in her mouth. The cool sensation brought a smile to her lips.

"So tell me," Mr. Cabbott said, tapping his pen on his small notepad. "Did you and your sister ever go to that shelter?"

"We did," Charlotte replied.

"I bet there were a lot of rough characters staying there," Mr. Cabbott observed.

"Horrible place to visit," Ruth added. "All kinds of people and children there. All of them looking quite sad about their disposition."

"Yes," Charlotte nodded, glancing over at Ruth. "It really was quite sad."

"Weren't you nervous about going to a place like that?" Mr. Cabbott asked.

"Nervous?" Charlotte asked.

"Why?" Ruth asked.

"Because the guy who runs it is one rough fella, as are some of the people who stay there," Mr. Cabbott observed. "I went there when I was working on my story. I know what it looks like and I know who lives there. Weren't you scared?"

"Heavens no," Charlotte said with a wave of her hand. "We knew we'd be warmly welcomed when we got there."

"How did you know that?" he asked.

"As I said," Charlotte smiled, "generosity opens many doors."

Charlotte noted how Mr. Cabbott poised his pen over a fresh sheet of paper in his notepad. His eyes focused on her, waiting for her to resume her story. She didn't want to disappoint him. She took a deep breath, collected her memories, and then began to tell the story of her trip to Holy Redeemer Shelter.

CHAPTER THIRTEEN: GUS MUNCHACK

In my opinion, the walk from St. John's Church to Holy Redeemer Shelter would be a daunting one for someone who was unfamiliar with downtown Washington. In fact, I would hazard a guess that most tourists would be downright intimidated by the sights they'd find on the way from my church to the shelter. The dark and cracked sidewalks they would have to follow. The crumbling buildings they'd pass along the way. The stray homeless people scattered along the streets arriving or departing from the shelter. One glimpse at their dirty clothes or rough demeanor would give someone pause. One whiff of their aroma would cause any tourist to hold their breath and turn away.

However, the route from St. John's Church to Holy Redeemer Shelter is one that my sister and I have travelled many times. It is a route we are familiar with after taking this path as young girls with our parents. I can still see myself jogging ahead of my parents, racing my sister home from church, giggling all the way. We'd always pass the building where the shelter is now located. Back in my youth I think it was a box factory, or so my mother told us. While the faces and sights along this route have changed considerably over the years, it was still a route that Ruth and I are comfortable taking.

We eventually stopped in front of a red brick building tucked along a side street. A bright white cross hung from the front of the building where we knew the shelter was located. When we got closer, I stepped in front of a black metal door fixed directly under the cross. The paint on the door was flaking in some spots and clearly in need of a fresh coat. Despite the rough appearance, I curled up my fingers and gave that worn out door two firm knocks.

When the door swung open, I found myself looking directly at a man's face. Before I could notice any details about his appearance, what stood out to me first was his expression. I couldn't decide if he looked like he'd just had a fight with someone, or if he was angry with me for having to open the door. After a few more seconds I also thought he looked tired, like he been up for twenty-four hours straight. I took a step back out and tried to force a smile to put the man at ease. The expression on his face didn't change. So there we stood, staring at each other, neither of us speaking. Our mutual silence gave me some time to notice a few more details about his appearance.

His hair was dark with streaks of gray along the sides. His beard, which touched the top of his chest, was more gray than black. A gold chain hung around his neck and a gold hoop earring dangled from one ear like a pirate. A tattoo of a spider was on the back of one hand. Given it was a spider tattoo, it made me a bit uneasy. The man's face looked rigid for a few seconds while he stared us down with blood shot eyes.

"You two need food or a bed?" he snapped.

"Neither," I quickly answered. "My name is Charlotte Dupree. This is my sister, Ruth."

Like magic, I watched that man's angry expression begin to change. The creases between his eyebrows slowly melted away. His lips actually appeared to push up the creases around the corners of his mouth, like he was attempting to smile.

"Are you the Dupree sisters?" the man asked.

"We might be," Ruth said, stepping behind me like she was expecting a punch to be thrown her way.

"You wouldn't happen to be from St. John's Church, would you?" he asked and he actually began to reveal a smile as much as his rigid face would allow.

"We are," I grinned, thinking I knew where this answer would lead.

"Well," the man grunted and the slight smile on his face turned into an expression of pure happiness. "This shelter made it through the winter because of you two. My name is Gus Munchack. I run this shelter. A few months back, when I saw that check you wrote to our shelter I told Reverend Simmons I'd never forget the names on it."

"So good of you to remember us," Ruth grinned.

"I don't forget big donations like that," Gus stated and his eyes grew wide as if he were still looking at the check. "When Reverend Simmons handed me that check for a few thousand dollars I couldn't believe it. When he explained that it was from you two so we could pay for our heater to get fixed back in November, I just laughed. You two were like angels last winter. I can't tell you how many people survived the cold because of your generosity."

"You can thank Reverend Simmons for that," Ruth smiled. "When he mentioned it at church…we knew we had to do something to help."

"Well," the man grunted and he stepped back from the doorway. "Forgive my manners, ladies. Would you two like to come in? I can show you around and you can see the heater that your money helped to repair."

Ruth looked at me and I could sense that she wasn't sure about the invitation. I looked at Gus. I'm a pretty good judge of character and I could sense that this rugged-looking gentleman was opening up a small piece of his heart to us by asking us into his shelter. Since he was running the shelter, I could tell his invitation was coming from a kind heart. I didn't want to reject his offer.

"What is your name again?" I asked.

"Gus Munchack," the man replied and he opened the door wider. "Now please come in and let me show you around."

"Do you think we should, sister?" Ruth whispered, grabbing me by the arm.

"We gave a large donation to this shelter last year and we talked about giving another one this year," I quietly answered. "I'm confident Gus will take good care of us so we'll be able to write more checks. Isn't that right, Gus?"

"I promise I won't let anything happen to my two golden geese," Gus laughed, opening the door wider. "Besides, we're not a prison, ladies. The people in here are either hungry or tired. You'll be safe."

There are moments when a person's heart can be glimpsed by the words they choose and the tone in their voice. In the few words that Gus spoke, something in my heart told me I could trust him. I took a deep breath and followed Gus inside with Ruth by my side.

I'd never been in a homeless shelter before, so I didn't quite know what to expert. The first thing I noticed was how the layout was small and confined. The rooms were narrow with very little space for privacy. The first room we stepped into appeared to be a living room at one time. A dusty old chandelier hung from the ceiling. It gave off dim shafts of light that illuminated a modestly-sized room filled with cots. My eyes moved around to the people who were stretched out on the cots. A few people were sleeping on them despite the fact it was bordering on noon. One cot simply looked like it had a pile of old dirty rags and blankets on it. When I saw the pile move, I realized it was actually a person wrapped in garments.

"Such a shame," Ruth sighed.

"It is a shame," Gus nodded. "But...we're blessed that God has allowed us to provide shelter for these people. I've talked to some folks in this shelter who have lost their way in life. Some folks used to have normal lives until a crisis came along and took everything away. The other night, I was talking to a fella who had an office job. Then he got laid off and couldn't pay the rent. Thanks to you two ladies, they all had a warm place to sleep last winter. Now that spring is here, and the weather is warming up, not every cot is being taken at night the way it was when the snows came."

"If you need more cots please let us know," I stated.

"I will," Gus nodded. "That's very generous."

"We came here today to ask you a question," Ruth began. "There was one young man we wanted to ask you about. He might have been one of those people who stayed here during the winter."

"I see lots of faces at that time of the year," Gus sighed. "Men, women, children. I don't put names with their faces. I don't even ask their names. We pray, they sleep here, and I try to give them a little something for breakfast before they leave. Usually it's pancakes cuz it helps them feel a little fuller when they go."

"Take a look at this picture," Charlotte said, handing Gus a small photo of a face from the church directory. "His name was Joseph Campbell. He was a very nice young man. He died last month on the steps of St. John's Church."

"Let me see," Gus said and his eyes lit up, like the conversation had turned down a familiar street. "That guy...yeah...I remember him. Polite. Had some manners to him. You see, not a lot of folks on the streets got manners which is why I remember him. He was a real nice guy...but he was a user."

"A user?" Ruth asked.

"He was hooked on drugs," Gus answered. "I remember praying with that kid and hearing him ask God to help him with his addiction. So…that's what he looked like all cleaned up? You say his name was Joseph. Round here I called him Shooter cuz that's how he liked his drugs…shooting them up in his veins. He was always carrying needles with him. I could tell when he came around here if he'd had a fix before he arrived. He'd be all nice and polite. If he didn't get a fix that day….let's just say he wasn't so good with his manners."

"So why did you let him in here if he was taking drugs?" I asked. "If someone came to my house I certainly wouldn't let them do what they pleased. They'd have rules to follow in my house."

"Well," Gus laughed. "This isn't a home, ma'am. This is a shelter. I'm not judging the folks who stay here. I'm just giving them a safe place to stay. I do have rules, though. One of my rules is that they can't bring drugs with them into my shelter. I check them for drugs before they set foot through the door and I keep my eyes open when I'm working. I gotta admit it's hard keeping an eye on everyone when they're here day and night, but I do my best."

"I'd suppose it must be a challenge," Ruth nodded. "If I ran a shelter…I think I'd only allow good, honest people to live in it. I think I could run a very good shelter."

"The city could always use another shelter around here, Miss Dupree," Gus grinned. "Lots of people could use another one in this city, if you're thinking of opening your own."

"Can I clarify something?" I sighed, interrupting my sister's train of thought on starting a shelter. "You said that Joseph was using drugs? The newspapers said that drugs were not involved in his death."

"I wasn't there when he died...but he was using drugs," Gus sighed.

"I'm surprised," I answered. "I know this man's family. They weren't giving him money anymore. How could he afford to buy drugs?"

"All I know is when I looked at his eyes, especially his pupils, I could tell he was using," Gus recalled.

"Really?" Ruth mumbled, stepping closer. "He didn't have a job and his family cut their ties with him. I wonder how he got drugs."

"Homeless folks with an addiction will do anything for money...if they're desperate enough," Gus explained. "Theft. Prostitution. A crap job no one else wants to do for crap money. Begging on a street corner. It wouldn't be hard for him to keep up with an addiction if he wanted to."

"All those things sound so unpleasant to me," Ruth sighed and she pulled her hand over her mouth.

I could tell that my sister was still seeing Joseph Campbell through the tainted lens of the past. She still saw him as that precious little boy who attended church with his family. I was less inclined to feel that way. I saw him as a man who made his choices. What bothered me was his fate. Some might feel that a homeless addict deserved this kind of fate by the bad choices he made. I certainly didn't share that opinion.

"I don't suppose you know who was selling him the drugs?" Ruth asked.

"Yes," I added. "Can you give us a name of any drug dealers around here?"

Gus looked around and took one small step closer to where Ruth and I were standing. In fact, he was so close I could smell cigarette smoke on him.

"Ladies," Gus began in a low soft voice. "You seem like nice people. I *know* you're both generous. Hearing you ask me about finding a drug dealer in this city…you don't want to mess around with that. You ladies don't want to get mixed up with finding a drug dealer to tell you what you want to hear. My experiences with drug dealers taught me that they're violent and not very nice to people who ask lots of questions."

I nodded at his warning when a thought flew into my head and out my lips before I could contain myself.

"Have you ever had a drug problem?" I asked.

"I don't do drugs, ma'am," Gus quickly replied.

"So how do you know so much about drug dealers and addiction?" I pressed.

"When I was younger," Gus sighed, "I…I had a weakness for drugs. I was an addict. God turned my life around and helped me to defeat the demons that crave drugs. So yes, another life ago, I was around drug dealers a good bit and I know how they are. You ladies would do best to stay away from them."

"We'll stick with getting our drugs from the pharmacy," I smiled. "Thank you for talking to us, Gus. If that furnace gives you any more problems, please let us know."

"Thank you for taking the time to stop down," Gus said, leading us back to the front door. "It really was nice to meet you both."

As we followed Gus back to the door, a large man appeared in the doorway. He was taller than Gus, wore a military jacket and had a cloth bag slung over his shoulder, and I guessed he was looking for a meal. He had a thick dark beard that wrapped down his cheeks and around his chin. I was surprised to see Gus hold out his hand and press firmly on the big man's chest when he tried to enter the shelter.

"You using today?" Gus asked.

"God won't let me," the man answered in a low gravely voice. "He told me in a dream that drugs are the devil's work. I ain't working for the devil no more."

"Show me your backpack," Gus demanded.

"That's my stuff!" the big man replied and his deep voice grew louder the way thunder does when it gets closer. "Nobody touches my stuff but me."

"Show me what you got or you aren't allowed in here!" Gus said in a very firm tone.

"You think you're God?" the man asked. "Only God talks to me that way and he only talks to me when I'm sleeping."

I watched as Gus's face slowly transformed to the same angry tired look that greeted Ruth and me when we first arrived.

"Look!" Gus said in a firm tone, "I run this place. I'm the boss here. I keep it clean for the folks who come here a lot. I got warm food and a bed in there. You're more than welcome to it, but you gotta show me you ain't carrying drugs in that bag."

The man glared at Gus. I swear I didn't see this homeless man's eyes move or one inch of his face change expression. Finally, he quietly slung his bag over his shoulder, turned and walked away. It really demonstrated to me Gus's passion for being a man of his word and not allowing drugs in his shelter. It also made me wonder if he ever turned away Joseph Campbell for the same reason.

Once we stepped out of the shelter, Ruth and I began our walk home. Neither one of us spoke to the other while we walked. There were plenty of things that I saw along the way to bring up as topics of conversation. A cardinal chirping from the ledge of a building. The clear blue sky. The warm sun. Yet, none of it seemed all that interesting after what we'd just seen. Eventually I suggested we go across the street to Lafayette Square. Together we found an empty bench, sat down and watched people pass by us.

"That really was quite sad," Ruth finally spoke up.

"What?" I asked, too lost in my own thoughts to hear what Ruth said.

"I said it was quite sad!" Ruth spoke a little louder. "Did you see that young mother in there with her child?"

"Yes," I nodded. "You're right, sister. It was quite sad. People make their choices in this world, Ruth. Sometimes those choices aren't the best ones."

"Sometimes the world makes choices for people too," Ruth countered.

I nodded in agreement as I watched a mother pass by pushing a baby stroller.

"I'm afraid Joseph made his choices," I commented, watching the stroller go by. "He chose drugs and he got addicted to them. It wasn't the world that got him hooked...it was Joseph."

"Poor Jo-Jo," Ruth sighed, squinting up at the sun.

"Yes," I nodded. "I'd still like to know how he was getting drugs...and clean needles. Now if what Gus said is correct, I don't think Joseph would have been spending money on both. I think he would have spent it on one or the other. With his addiction, he was probably spending every cent he had on drugs. Which makes me wonder where he was getting his clean needles from."

We grew silent on the matter and began to watch the activity that filled the park at Lafayette Square. What caught my eye were the children. While my sister and I hadn't been fortunate enough to marry or have children, I often find the mannerisms of young children to be quite fascinating. They have an uninhibited way about themselves, which I notice in how they talk and how they play.

That day at the park I watched one boy in particular, who had bright golden curls and a smile that lit up his face. I noticed how much he laughed while he ran. It just made me smile to see it. Then I thought of young Joseph at this age and I wished time had left him remain as a boy so he never had to grow up.

CHAPTER FOURTEEN: A PLACE TO REFLECT

A few days later, Ruth and I went to one of our favorite places to be during the warmer months—the reflecting pool near the Lincoln Memorial. Now I don't know about Ruth, but for me it's a place that is a perfect barometer for measuring the level of activity in the city.

By day, the reflecting pool is a hub of activity. It's like watching a pocket watch run at full clip. School buses drive by. Young school children linger by the reflecting pool in loud packs with their teachers. Tourists snap pictures of how the pool captures the image of the Washington Monument before charging off to other landmarks. Those are just some of the reasons why people tend to walk at a brisk pace along the paths beside the reflecting pool. Time is precious to them. Visiting Washington for the day requires them to move quickly to get to all the museums, the memorials, and the other sites tourists like to see. Yet, when the sun goes down, a different kind of pace settles over the area around the reflecting pool.

At dusk, the crowds begin to thin out. School groups have boarded their buses and left for home. Tourists are safely back on the highway. The majority of people who remain around the reflecting pool in the evening hours are people who live in the city.

These people walk at a much slower pace. There is less urgency to how they move and how they act. In my opinion, they're there to soak in the milky golden sunset, the hush of the evening and the calm that settles over the city after another busy day. I think they come out to enjoy the lavender light that illuminates the town at sunset. I also think they enjoy how peach-colored clouds tend to reflect perfectly off the water.

I can't speak for my sister, but for my money this is the Washington I grew up to love. Not the Washington that's filled with ambitious people who move at a frenetic pace and ignore cherry blossoms or peerless blue skies. My Washington can best be enjoyed in the evenings, when the colors are richer and the pace of the town winds down and people have time to reflect on the beauty that surrounds them.

One evening, my sister and I enjoyed a lovely dinner at a bistro not far from our house. Looking out the window while we dined, the sky was beginning to take on hints of pink and gold. When we finished our meals we quickly paid our bill, hailed a cab, and instructed the driver to take us to the reflecting pool by the Lincoln Memorial to watch the sky grow golden, the clouds turn plum colored while the sun set.

Once there we found a bench by the reflecting pool to watch some people and marvel at the colors of the evening. With gold and violet light flickering off the water, my thoughts turned back to the homeless shelter. Gus never knew Joseph as a young man. He never knew Joseph when he was filled with promise. Gus only knew him as a homeless man who died like most homeless people do; from the elements of winter, or from being mugged, or from a drug overdose. It's easy in this town of important people to feel numb about what happens to the homeless. It's easier to keep an eye on the White House or the Capital Building and get caught up in the lives of important people who live in Washington, rather than think of the homeless.

"Who would help him?" I finally asked my sister.

"Who?" Ruth asked.

"Joseph," I stated, glancing over at Ruth. "Who was giving him needles? Who was giving him money for drugs?"

"The family cut him off," Ruth answered. "Maybe a friend? Perhaps he was doing a job for someone to earn the money…or begging for it."

"Maybe," I sighed. "I just don't see Joseph as a beggar. You grow up a Campbell…you're too proud to beg, in my opinion."

"Do you remember him coming to church with his family?" Ruth asked and she smiled and turned her eyes up to the pink and purple clouds overhead. "He was a sweet boy, with dark hair combed to the side and dark brown eyes that seemed to tickle your heart when he looked at you. He was truly a boy of innocence. Yet, somewhere along the way that innocence was lost."

"We all lose that innocence," I sighed. "It's a shame that life works that way."

My eyes turned to the reflecting pool. The water glowed with golden light that lapped before us. I thought about life and how we all lose our innocence, some more dramatically than others. I watched the water move and change colors and turn from golden to violet, like the sky. I tried to quiet my thoughts. Then I heard voices in the distance laughing loudly. My eyes turned to see two small boys running towards a tree. They were quite young, skipping and pointing wildly at a nearby tree. When they reached it, I watched them jump for a branch to try to climb up. After a few hops, it became clear that the tree was too tall for either boy to conquer.

Then I saw the one boy grab the other boy by the waist and lift him up. The boy being lifted stretched and finally managed to grab hold of the branch. Just as he was pulling himself up, a young woman I guessed was the boys' mother came over. She pulled her one son from the branch then pointed her finger at both boys and began to scold them.

"That mother doesn't look too happy," I chuckled.

"Yes," Ruth said. "You put two brothers together and you don't know what they're capable of doing."

Her words made me pause for a moment before thinking about Joseph again.

"You're right, sister," I agreed. "The bond between brothers can be quite close. Perhaps we should track down Joseph's brothers to see how they're dealing with their grief."

CHAPTER FIFTEEN: BROTHERS

When we returned home from watching such a lovely sunset, we began to prepare for a late dinner. On this particular evening it was Ruth's turn to cook. She prepared a pasta dish with Alfredo sauce, fresh broccoli, chicken and dried tomatoes. The smell lingered in every room and I found my mouth about to water no matter what I was doing or where I went in our house.

When Ruth announced that dinner was ready, I couldn't wait to get to the kitchen and stick a forkful of pasta in my mouth. After one bite, the seasoning on the chicken and the flavor from the sauce danced around on my tongue in such a playful way it made me smile. The meal was simply a pleasure to eat. Once I settled into the meal my mind began to reflect on the day.

"It was a good day, sister," I finally sighed.

"I quite enjoyed our walk by the reflecting pool," Ruth replied before taking a bite of a dinner roll. "There were a lot of people out there today."

"It was very busy." I smiled and nodded. "It was nice to see so many people out enjoying the evening. I do so love watching the children play. Especially those two boys who were trying to climb up that tree."

"Those two boys looked like a couple of rascals to me," Ruth giggled.

"They did," I replied before taking a bite of my dinner roll. "I think they were brothers."

"What makes you think that?" Ruth asked. "I mean I saw the mother scolding one of the boys, but the other one could have been a friend."

"I could tell they were brothers by the way they worked together," I observed. "I remember how they were helping each other...how they were talking to each other. It just reminded me of how brothers help one another no matter what the challenge. When one brother struggles, the other brother is always there to lend a hand. That's how I think life works."

"So true, Charlotte," Ruth replied. "Kind of like us."

"Indeed," I smiled.

We raised our water glasses and tapped them together in a spontaneous toast.

"Siblings always make a good team, don't they?" Ruth sighed.

"I've been thinking about that a lot since we left the park," I began before taking a sip of my water. "You see, Ruth, I've been thinking about how most brothers and sisters tend to help each other. The Campbells are a close family. Do you think Joseph's brothers would just cut him off as easily as their father did? I mean if mother would have tossed me out on the street, would you have turned your back on me and left me to scrounge just because mother said to?"

"Of course not!" Ruth snapped. "You know I'm always there to help you."

"Precisely my point," I said. "I find it hard to believe Joseph's brothers and sister had no contact with him when he left. They would have wanted to help...like you would with me."

"Well, he was staying at that homeless shelter," Ruth pointed out. "We know he wasn't just sleeping in an alley."

"And yet he had money for drugs," I quickly responded. "Despite what that nice man said at the shelter, when one comes from a family of privilege one doesn't think of creative ways to earn money. One feels entitled to it. Joseph grew up in a family where he was given everything he wanted. I told you I suspected someone was giving him money. I'm beginning to think it was someone from within the family."

"You think someone…wanted him to keep using drugs?" Ruth asked.

"I think someone wanted to help him," I replied. "I don't think they were buying drugs for him…but I think they were giving Joseph money because they were supporting a family member in trouble. Now Miles cut Joseph off from the family, so I know the money wasn't coming from him. As for his wife, we've known Natalie for a long time. She certainly wouldn't want Joseph on drugs. I know Grace is the older sister, but she has a new husband so I think it would be hard for her to slip away to track down Joseph. That leaves Thomas and Ethan as the two people who could have been coming down to the shelter to see Ethan."

"Brothers helping a brother," Ruth replied. "Like those boys in the tree."

"Thomas and Ethan Campbell aren't married," I continued. "From what I gather they're pretty much on their own. One of them is a professor and the other runs an art gallery. Their schedules are pretty unconventional which is why I think it would be quite easy for either one of them to slip away to help their brother."

"They always were close," Ruth mumbled. "Do you remember all the activities the Campbell sons were involved in together as boys? They were quite close growing up. Do you remember when they were Boy Scouts?"

"They looked so sharp in their Scout uniforms back then," I said and a faint image of the Campbell boys' faces flickered in my mind the way a dying candle reflects off something with a faint gold hue.

"I remember those boys when they were in our church's youth groups, too," Ruth said. "Remember when they were teens? I can easily recall the one time they organized a Bingo Night to raise funds for the local chapter of the Humane Society. I can still see Thomas stepping to the front of the church more than once to ask the congregation for their support in raising funds. Thomas was always such a well-spoken young man. He really looked after Ethan and Joseph."

"I believe Thomas is an economics professor at George Washington University," I said.

"Oh, yes," Ruth nodded. "I forgot about that."

"He's been there for a few years, now," I continued.

"I can remember how proud his parents were to share that news," Ruth nodded.

"I'd suppose it would be easy to contact the college and get his schedule," I suggested. "Perhaps we could line up an appointment with him."

"That's a splendid idea, sister," Ruth replied.

"It certainly would be a pleasant surprise for him!" I laughed. "I wonder when the last time was he met with two people in his office who weren't in their twenties."

"I have some sympathy cards laying around here somewhere," Ruth stated, her eyes darting around the room. "Maybe we should sign one and deliver it to Thomas."

"A thoughtful gesture is always appreciated," I replied.

Without hesitation, our plan was in motion. Ruth found a card and signed it while I called the college. After sitting on hold numerous times, I was finally able to reach a secretary in the Economics Department. Quite by luck she was able to secure us an appointment for the following day.

The next morning we rose early, dressed like we were going to church, then chatted over breakfast about what we would and wouldn't ask Thomas. In fact we were so caught up in discussing our plan that the newspaper, which was always part of our morning routine, laid untouched on the counter.

As soon as we finished breakfast, we called for a taxi and quickly grabbed our purses and left. It was an enjoyable ride to George Washington University. The taxi driver was rather friendly and more than willing to engage us in some small talk about the weather and the unreasonable flow of traffic for this time of the morning. He told us more than once about how Congress had just returned from a break and that the increased number of cars out and about in the city was a sign that Congress was back in session again.

A short ten-minute drive from our house to George Washington University became a bit longer, but we eventually arrived with a few minutes to spare for our appointment.

The college itself has a wonderful history. The school is the product of an idea from George Washington himself to establish a college within the nation's capital. Thanks to President James Monroe, the idea came to fruition when students began to arrive for classes in 1821.

When Ruth and I stepped out of the cab, we walked by a large metal bust of George Washington mounted on a tall slab of granite. It was a clear indication that we were entering the campus. We followed the red-bricked walkways that led us by patches of green grass, full green trees, and tall red-brick buildings looming in the distance. Ruth held her directions that she'd written down, in order to know which red-brick building would lead us to Thomas.

"Look at them," Ruth sighed, glancing around at the young faces walking by us. "Look at their eyes. Look at the way they look. They have their whole future in front of them and they look like they can't wait to live it."

"All the students look like that," I said. "They walk so fast, they talk to each other with such…conviction, and they have such an energy about them. I think I'd like to come back to college, Ruth. I think this kind of energy might be fun to be around for a semester."

"We'd make quite a scene if we enrolled in a class at our age," Ruth giggled.

"I wonder if we'd be invited to any parties?" I giggled back.

Using the directions that Ruth had written down, and a few thoughtful directions from students, we managed to find a two-story building that reminded me of a single-family home more than offices. A sign on the porch to the building indicated that it was indeed home to the Economics Department. So we walked inside, took some narrow steps up to the second floor, and moved down a dark hallway with doors on either side. Each door had a nameplate, telling us which Economics' professor was behind which door. When we saw the name Thomas Campbell, I felt quite confident in opening the door.

Behind the door we found a very small room, with Thomas sitting behind a dark wood desk correcting papers by a desk lamp that cast a dim light for him to read. The smell of hot tea dripped from the air and I spotted a mug on his desk with steam twirling up. Behind him, a narrow window let in a measured amount of light that was bright enough to provide some illumination, but not much else. I thought it looked more like a walk-in closet than an office for a tenured faculty member.

"Not very glamorous," Ruth whispered.

"This isn't what I envisioned," I whispered back.

When Thomas looked up, his head tilted to the side and a grin crept across his face. He looked happy, but then his eyebrows also sank down as he took off his reading glasses. I could tell he was a bit confused. When he stood up, he appeared as tall and as slender as he looked at the funeral. His brown hair appeared darker in the room and his ponytail dangled over his shoulder as he walked around his desk.

"Well, this is a welcome surprise!" Thomas smiled and he gave both of us a hug. "What on earth brings you two ladies here? Are you lost?"

"We're right where we want to be," I smiled before giving Thomas another quick hug.

"It's nice to see you two." Thomas grinned. His eyes dipped down to check his wrist watch. "I'm sorry to make this brief, but I have an appointment coming any minute."

"That's us," I said.

"Yes, we're your appointment," Ruth added.

"You?" Thomas asked, the grin on his face being replaced with an even more confused expression.

"Your secretary is so sweet," I explained. "I called here yesterday. She couldn't say no to me after I was finished talking with her. She said I sounded just like her grandmother with all the questions I asked. Such a sweet thing to fit us in with an appointment on such short notice."

"Charlotte, you do have a way of charming people," Ruth said.

"I agree." Thomas laughed and he gripped the back of his wooden chair behind his desk. "Both of you ladies can charm with the best of them. Please, sit down."

Ruth and I settled into two wooden chairs that matched the color of Thomas's desk. Thomas took a sip from a steaming mug and quickly remembered his manners.

"Would the two of you like some hot tea?" he asked.

"No, thank you," I replied.

"None for me," Ruth mumbled.

"Very well," Thomas said before taking another sip. "I find that warm tea keeps my throat loose. Giving so many lectures everyday is hard on my voice."

"You don't have to give me an excuse to drink tea," I smiled. "I have at least one cup every day. Sometimes with breakfast, sometimes in the afternoon."

Thomas nodded politely at my words. I couldn't help but think it was the same nod he probably gives every student who visits him to solicit advice or guidance.

"So you made an appointment...to see me?" Thomas asked, slowly moving behind his desk and lowering his narrow frame into his chair. "What can I do for you?"

"Thomas, we've known your family for many years," I began. "To be blunt, Ruth and I simply can't understand why your brother was living on his own. Your family has always been close and to see one of you living off the streets...well...it just doesn't make sense to us. Did it bother you knowing that he was homeless?"

"Shouldn't you be talking to mother about this?" Thomas asked, nervously rubbing his large hands together as if he were warming up by a fire.

"Your mother is in mourning," Ruth pointed out. "We tried to talk to her, Thomas, but it's just too difficult for her right now."

Thomas got up and closed the door to his office. He turned, looked at both of us and then walked back to his seat. He sat there staring at his desk in what appeared to be an attempt to think about whether to respond to us or not.

"The truth will set you free, but first it will make you miserable," Ruth spoke up.

"What?" Thomas asked, clearly lost in his thoughts.

"It's a quote from President James Garfield," Ruth explained. "A quote that just seems appropriate for the moment."

"Look, the last few years of my brother's life were tough," Thomas began. He drummed his fingers on his desk while he thought about what words to use next. "We...we watched Joey spiral down into drug addiction. He completed a treatment program but lapsed again. We all wanted to help, but dad said he had to hit rock bottom before he could help himself. Dad told all of us to not help Joseph. To let him suffer. So we stepped back and did what he said."

"That must have been hard for you to let your brother go like that," I sighed.

"The brother I knew was gone long before he was homeless," Thomas said with a very matter-of-fact tone and expression. He slipped his reading glasses off and rubbed his eyes the way someone does when they're tired. "My brother and I used to do so much together...and then all of a sudden Joey just wanted to hang out with the kind of people he could buy drugs from. The day I learned he'd died...I wasn't upset...I was relieved for Joey."

"Why would you say that?" I asked.

"It seemed to me Joey was out of our lives long before this happened," Thomas began and he pointed across his desk to Ruth and me. "We were close...like you two. We played golf together when we were younger. We enjoyed the same movies as we got older. When we went to college we'd call each other every day. And then suddenly, it was all taken away from me.

My world changed and...I couldn't get it back. He was off in another world....so I just got on with my life. He lived on the streets for months...and I never heard from him. To me...it was like he was already gone long before his body died."

"That must have been a very difficult thing to realize," I said.

Thomas didn't reply to my observation. He simply kept his hands on his desk, his eyes cast down. Finally, he reached over to a picture frame that sat at on one side of his desk. He handed the frame to Ruth and me. We looked to find a picture of Joseph and Thomas looking quite sharp in suits and ties.

"That's the Joey I remember," Thomas mumbled, pointing at the frame. "That's my bro...and I miss him every day."

When we finished, Thomas was kind enough to call us a cab. Before we left his tiny office, we hugged him one more time and offered him our condolences again. When you hug children that you've known all of your life, it's as close as I can imagine to hugging your own child.

Walking along the walkways that crisscrossed around the campus, I couldn't help but smile again at the young people around us. The purpose in their walk. The conversations I heard and the tone in their voices while they spoke. Even in looking at their faces when I passed, I could see the promise in their eyes. The promise of youth. The promise of better things that lie ahead in the future. The kind of things that Joseph used to think about before he became an addict.

In a few minutes, the taxi ride home became slower, thanks to more traffic. I stared out the window at the cars around us and reflected on what Thomas had said.

"He didn't seem all that upset about Jo-Jo," Ruth remarked.

"You know, even as a child, Thomas was always fairly reserved," I recalled.

"That is true," Ruth replied. "He sounded as though he was able to rationalize his feelings for Joseph a long time ago. Not the way I'd expect a brother to feel towards another brother."

"He may not have been in tears but he misses Joseph," I sighed. "You can tell, especially by how he keeps that picture on his desk. How he wanted us to see it. He sees his brother's face everyday at work. That speaks volumes to me. Such a shame Joseph had to wrestle with addiction."

"We never had a family member with an addiction problem, did we?" Ruth pointed out.

"Father did drink a good bit," I recalled. "Mother always called it social drinking."

"Yes," Ruth said, "plus he only drank in the evenings. Never in the mornings or the afternoons. He could control his love for alcohol. I get the impression Joseph didn't have that kind of....discipline."

"I agree," I smiled.

"So that leaves Ethan," Ruth replied.

"Yes...Ethan," I said, glancing out the window of the taxi.

"And what do you know about him? What is Ethan up to these days?" Ruth asked.

"Grace said he runs an art gallery on the north side of town," I stated. "I made some calls and found that the gallery has a new collection opening this weekend. They're also having a special event to celebrate the opening. I was able to get us some tickets for the event."

"So we have a date?" Ruth asked.

"Saturday night…we will be sipping champagne and enjoying a gallery opening," I nodded. "I'm quite looking forward to it. It's been a long time since you and I have been to an art gallery."

"Yes," Ruth added, "and don't forget about Ethan. That's why we're doing this…to talk to Ethan."

I nodded at what would be the most important detail of the night.

CHAPTER SIXTEEN: THE PORTRAIT OF A BROTHER

When the weekend arrived, Ruth and I called a taxi and took a short ride to the Edison Gallery, a small privately run art gallery that we'd never been to before. Ruth and I have always enjoyed art and have been to many galleries in Washington over the years. However, neither of us knew much about the Edison Gallery so we were curious to see it.

While we drove, it gave me time to think about how, from an early age, our mother took us to the best art galleries in the city. She enjoyed taking us to see collections at museums that she deemed worthy of our attention. I can clearly remember my first gallery trip, which was to see a collection of Claude Monet's works of his gardens. On that first trip, I remember how my mother gently took my hand and walked me away from the front of the painting. She moved me to the side of some of the work and began to point out the strokes of paint layered on the canvas. She explained that there are many layers to things in life and to try to find the beauty in those details. Growing up, mother gave us a deep appreciation for art. When we got older, we kept our passion for art alive.

During the course of a year, Ruth and I try to get to major galleries like the Freer Gallery, the Long View Gallery and, of course, the National Gallery of Art. The smaller ones slip by us, which is what made this venture to Ethan's gallery so interesting.

When our taxi finally pulled up at the Edison Gallery, Ruth and I stepped out to find a building that, from the outside, resembled a diner more than a place to display art. Suddenly the front door to the building opened and a young lady with bright pink hair and a silver ring through her nose stepped out to leave the gallery.

"I think one of the displays is escaping," Ruth laughed.

"Hush!" I replied. "You know how kids are these days. They'll do practically anything to express themselves...whether it's tasteful or not."

"I don't have a good feeling about this gallery, sister," Ruth said, waving her finger in the air. "This had better be a traditional collection, Charlotte. You know I don't like the modern works. If they have anything nude or crude in there I will simply walk out...and I'll tell Ethan as much before I leave."

"That's fine," I nodded. "Remember why we're here, Ruth. We're not here to critique the gallery or what art Ethan chooses to display. We're here to talk to Ethan about his brother. And remember, he's the sensitive one in the family so don't say anything to upset him."

"Why are you telling me that?" Ruth asked.

"Because you're always more...direct with your words," I explained. "Mother always said you needed more tact and sometimes I see her point."

"Hogwash!" Ruth replied. "I'm certain it will be an exciting event for Ethan. I wouldn't dream of saying anything to ruin it for him."

I quietly nodded in agreement with Ruth's vow. Having known Ethan Campbell for as long as I have, I know this was the same person who loved chasing butterflies after church as a boy. The same Ethan who would cry after the Christmas service was over because he didn't want the holidays to end. He was always sensitive growing up and I knew that deep down inside of the man he was today, I suspected that there was still some of that boy inside of his heart.

When we stepped inside the Edison Gallery, the first thing I noticed was a harpist and violinist playing music that filled the air with magic. A white marble floor spread out before us, while almond-colored walls wrapped around the scenery. Lighting fell from above, perfectly accenting the works on display. Ruth and I walked from one room to the next, admiring the paintings of various landscapes by an artist named Thomas Hill.

"I think this gallery is much bigger on the inside," Ruth whispered.

"You're right, sister," I nodded and I couldn't help but notice all the young couples flowing around us. "Even with such a good turnout, I don't feel the least bit crowded."

Together Ruth and I moved through about five rooms, admiring the works on display and talking about the people we spied. We eventually worked our way to a smaller room in the very back of the gallery. That's where we found Ethan Campbell standing with a glass of wine.

He wore a dark suit and his brown hair was neatly trimmed. He was chatting with two young assistants about responsibilities they would need to follow through on for the evening. A young lady lingered by Ethan's side, with a tablet and a phone in either hand. All in all, he looked quite important to anyone who would have laid eyes on him. However, when he looked at me I could see his face change. I could see the rigid expression on his face melt into a more familiar look that I knew belonged to the boy and not the man. He stepped away from the people surrounding him and walked right up to us.

"Hello, Ethan," I sighed.

He put his wine glass down, stepped up to us and wrapped his arms around my shoulders and hugged me harder than I'd been hugged in a long time. He then stepped away from me and did the same thing to Ruth. I could tell Ethan was squeezing her tightly by the way Ruth looked at me.

"So good to see both of you," Ethan said and he stepped back and looked at Ruth and me with a little grin on his face that reminded me of a little boy smile. "I saw both of you at the funeral and I wanted to talk but...I was just too upset. It was so nice of you to come to the funeral. What brings the two of you down to this side of town?"

"We're here for the opening," I fibbed. "Thomas Hill is one of our favorite artists. It was just a pleasant surprise to discover you work here."

"Really?" Ethan said and he pushed his thick black hair to the side. "You love Hill's paintings?"

"How could anyone not appreciate a beautiful landscape?" I asked.

"That is true," Ethan said, turning to a painting of what I think was a work entitled *El Capitan*. "The details in this work are simply exquisite."

"It is a nice piece," I said and turned to Ruth. "What do you think, sister?"

"Lovely as a postcard from God," Ruth smiled.

"Yes...God..." I started to say but my tongue didn't know what else to do and I found my eyes being drawn right back to the painting.

"We're sorry about your brother," I finally said. "There's nothing more we can say on the matter, Ethan. We came here to look at paintings and we just wanted you to know how very sorry we are."

"Thank you," Ethan mumbled.

"Well," I smiled, taking one small step back. "You must have a lot to do, please don't let us keep you from your work."

"I pay people to do the work," Ethan stated. "I'm here to greet people and give this gallery a face. I like that part of my job. The number of phone calls, dinner engagements, travel and meetings all to land this collection for a few weeks...that's the part of running a gallery I don't care for all that much."

"It's a shame you couldn't have gotten Joseph a job here," Ruth said, cutting to the heart of the matter with a few quick words. "He always had such a nice smile."

"He was in no condition to work...anywhere," Ethan quickly pointed out.

I waited for Ethan to say more, but he grew silent and simply looked at us. I thought it was interesting how Ethan didn't elaborate on any of his comments about his brother. He gave a very straightforward answer and that seemed to be enough for him. Unlike Thomas and Grace, Ethan wasn't going to provide us with any insight into his thoughts about his brother. Perhaps he felt it wasn't the right occasion. Maybe he was too focused on the evening's activities to dwell on the conversation.

"Ethan," I finally said, stepping a little closer to him in an attempt to break the silence. "When your father kicked Joseph out of the house...what did you think?"

"Of course I was upset," Ethan replied, his eyes looking around the room. "I always thought Joseph could beat his addiction. He just needed people to support him. When dad sent him away, I understood why but I didn't think it was going to help Joseph with his problem. I felt like dad was just...closing the door on Joseph."

"Mr. Campbell!" a young girl said. I looked to see a rail thin girl with hot pink hair step up next to Ethan before sticking a small phone in his face. "It's that one art dealer you've been trying to reach."

Ethan nodded, grabbed the phone and took a deep breath. He then turned and walked away without so much as a glance at Ruth and myself. It was like in that second, he flipped a switch and stopped being a mourning brother and turned into the curator of the gallery again.

"The brother who cared," I whispered.

"What?" Ruth asked.

"I always thought Ethan was the brother who cared," I observed. "Now I'm not so sure."

"Why do you say that?" Ruth asked.

"Come here," I said, reaching out and grabbing Ruth by the arm and pulling her through the many bodies that circulated around the gallery.

"Charlotte!" I heard Ruth say. "Where are we going? Are you looking for the bathroom? Is that why you're pulling me along with you?"

"When we first arrived, I was looking around and I found Ethan's office," I said, weaving my way to the very back of the gallery.

"So that's where you went when you left me," Ruth stated.

"I was looking for something for us to drink when I found it," I replied, pulling Ruth behind me. "Once I arrived at the back of the building I saw some nondescript offices. I also spotted a door with Ethan's name on it and I opened the door."

"Charlotte!" Ruth scolded and she pulled her hand from mine. "If you're taking me to Ethan's office...well, you can forget about it. We're going to get in trouble!"

"No, we won't!" I said and I took her hand and pulled her into Ethan's office with me.

"We're going to get in trouble," Ruth grumbled.

"No we won't," I replied, flicking on the lights. "Besides, it's a big opening and Ethan and his colleagues are quite busy out there."

I stepped behind Ethan's desk and scanned the items on the desk. I carefully walked around the small office, noting what items were on the walls, on the filing cabinets, on the windowsills. Then I looked at Ruth. Her eyes appeared to be twice their size and her head kept turning from me to the doorway.

"We're going to get caught," Ruth hissed with a soft voice. "Let's get out of here."

"Fine…I'm done," I said, walking by Ruth and out of the office. I flicked the lights off and we quickly immersed ourselves in with the throngs of people packing the gallery.

"So what was that all about?" Ruth demanded.

"I'll tell you later," I replied.

So we stuck around the gallery for the rest of the evening. We enjoyed the music. We sipped champagne. We strolled around and admired the many works of art on display. While we looked at the beautiful works, we occasionally saw couples we knew enjoying the festivities.

Of course, Ruth and I never miss a chance to socialize. We quickly spoke with the ladies we knew and began to comment on the works we saw. We shared our passion for art with a few couples that were kind enough to chat with us. We admired Ethan's intellectual knowledge on art and the many comments he made to his guests throughout the evening.

By the end of the evening, Ruth and I were happy that the opening was a success for Ethan. Things moved smoothly. Employees were discreet. The paintings were breathtaking. In all, the opening proved quite successful because of one man behind the scenes. Ethan clearly took the time to plan every detail and manage every employee to perfection. All in all, Ruth and I both thought the evening was a success for the gallery and Ethan.

By the end of the night, Ruth and I bid Ethan a farewell and took a taxi home. We weren't in the cab more than a minute before Ruth spoke up.

"So why were you snooping in Ethan's office?" Ruth asked with a hint of anger in her voice. "It's just like when we were girls, Charlotte, you'd always get me to join you to do things that got us in trouble with mother. You're still a bad influence."

"You sound like mother," I laughed. "Scolding me for doing something wrong."

"Maybe I am," Ruth answered. "Tell me you had a good reason for snooping around Ethan's office."

"I wasn't snooping," I said with a defensive tone in my voice. "I knew exactly what I was looking for. You see, sister, when you have a purpose to what you do it's not snooping."

"So what do you call it?" Ruth said.

"Looking for a missing detail," I answered.

"And what detail was that?" Ruth asked.

"I thought it was interesting how tight-lipped Ethan was about Joseph," I said, glancing out the window of our cab. "I expected more words and more emotion from him."

"So?" Ruth said. "That doesn't explain us breaking into his office."

"I went to his office to look around. Did you notice that Ethan doesn't even have one picture of Joseph in his office? Not on his desk. Not on the walls. Not even on a shelf or filing cabinet."

"Sorry I didn't notice...I was too busy being your lookout," Ruth answered.

"Well, he doesn't," I answered. "You remember, Thomas was quite proud of the picture he had of Joseph on his desk. If you died, Ruth, I'd definitely keep a picture of you around too. Why doesn't Ethan have a picture of his brother?"

"People mourn in different ways," Ruth sighed.

"Perhaps," I said while my mind raced with possibilities for the way Ethan spoke and why there was no picture of Joseph to be found.

"So what do you think that means?' Ruth asked.

"I don't know," I said before turning my eyes out the cab window to the skyline of Washington. The lights of the city flickered by my window while I reflected on everything that had happened this evening. We both remained silent for the ride home.

CHAPTER SEVENTEEN: SUSPICIONS ABOUT MR. MUNCHACK

On Monday, Ruth and I decided to have Reverend Simmons over for lunch. We extended the invitation after church on Sunday and were not surprised when he accepted the invitation without hesitation. Over the years, Reverend Simmons has never been one to turn down our invitations for tea, lunch, or dinner. Sometimes I wonder if it's because of how we prepare the food, or out of sympathy for visiting the elderly, or if it's simply because he's a big man with a healthy appetite.

"So nice of you to have me over, ladies," Reverend Simmons said when we greeted him at the door.

"It's always nice to receive a guest," I quickly answered, taking his coat when he stepped into our home. "You know this house was built for socializing. Our mother used to have enormous parties here. My sister and I have hosted our share of social engagements over the years, too. We've even done some fundraising for various candidates. However, as we've gotten older, the house has become quieter. Most of our socializing occurs outside of these walls now. You know, luncheons, banquets, that sort of thing. Having a guest like you over is...good for us. It helps us keep busy."

"I'd suppose you two ladies are busy enough going from one social function to the next," Reverend Simmons pointed out while he followed Ruth and me into our sitting room.

"There is one day out of the week we try to keep free from social obligations," Ruth pointed out and she handed him a small cup of hot tea, prepared the way she knew he liked it.

"Yes," I chimed in. "We try to make Monday our one day of the week to stick around the house. In our home, we call Monday, "Mop Up Day" because that's when we do some cleaning and organizing around here. There was a time when we were young and working and we were so busy with social obligations that we didn't even bother to clean up. In fact, we used to pay a maid to come and clean our house back in those days. However, as we got older we learned that there is something satisfying about doing the work ourselves."

"Although mother would have a different opinion on that," Ruth added.

"Yes, mother quite enjoyed the company of her maids until the hour she died," I said.

"So Monday is your cleaning day?" Reverend Simmons asked before taking another sip of his tea.

"That's right." I nodded. "In the morning Ruth does the dusting while I mop the floors. We turn up the music of Johann Christian Bach and flutter around the house like two busy birds. We run a load of laundry, clean out any old food from our pantry, and draw up a shopping list for meals for the week. Since it's just the two of us, it's a short list."

"Although lately you've been eating more than me," Ruth observed.

"Hush!" I scolded before turning back to our guest. "Reverend Simmons isn't interested in my eating habits!"

"I was just making an observation," Ruth defended.

"Later in the day," I continued, "we move on to playing music by Mozart. It keeps me calm while I write out the bills for the month and balance my checkbook. Ruth usually folds the laundry and then we settle in for a cup of tea and look around at the work we've accomplished. Being able to see the fruits of one's labor, in my opinion, is the best result of Mop Up Day."

"Well," Reverend Simmons laughed, "I should have you two ladies over to my house. Since my wife died I don't clean the house as often as she did."

"It's something we enjoy doing together," Ruth said and her eyes turned in my direction.

"So what shall we talk about today, ladies?" Reverend Simmons asked. "The scripture readings from Sunday? The church finances? I've known you two long enough to know that you have a very specific concern on your minds when you invite me here...and it's not house cleaning. What is your concern, ladies?"

"The homeless shelter," I quickly replied. "The one that our church sponsors."

"Holy Redeemer," Reverend Simmons said.

"Yes," I replied. "You see, reverend, my sister and I visited there the other day. We wanted to see the heating system we paid to fix and it looked quite nice. The man who runs the shelter was very grateful when he spoke to us."

"As well he should be," Reverend Simmons pointed out. "It was a very cold winter this year. What you ladies did was very generous. I think we'll enjoy this spring after so many dark cold days."

"Indeed," I said. "Now back to that man...the one who runs the shelter. What is his name again?"

"Gus Munchack," he answered.

"Yes," I replied. "Mr. Munchack said some of the people who stay there have drug addictions. Does our church know this?"

"Drugs aren't allowed inside the shelter," Reverend Simmons explained. "Gus is very adamant about that.

It's something we agreed on before we started to support the shelter. People are free to stay at Holy Redeemer...but they can't bring drugs inside the shelter."

"Joseph Campbell was on drugs when he stayed there," I replied. "Gus said he knew that he was on drugs, but he didn't know where Joseph was buying them. I was wondering if it was possible that someone inside the shelter was selling him the drugs to make money."

"Do you trust this Gus fellow?" Ruth finally asked in a very direct tone. "He seems like he's got lots of reasons to need money there. Would he be selling drugs?"

"You think Gus Munchack is selling drugs?" Reverend Simmons laughed. "I've known Gus for many years, ladies. He comes to church quite a bit for guidance. We pray together on a good many things. I don't think he'd be selling drugs."

"When I think of a shelter," I started to explain, "I think of strangers moving in and out of a place. Joseph was always a shy boy. He was not very outgoing. I just can't see him approaching strangers on the street, or in a shelter, to ask them for money, drugs, or clean needles. The more I think about it the more it just doesn't make sense to me."

"Perhaps the boy you knew had become just another hard luck case," Reverend Simmons observed. "Addiction changes people, Charlotte."

"I can't begin to tell you how many times in the evening Charlotte and I watch the late news and shake our heads at the sad stories presented," Ruth began. "So many people are arrested over drugs. So many people shot or killed over drugs. It really is quite a shame."

"Be that as it may, ladies, I don't think Gus is a drug dealer," Reverend Simmons said.

Ruth and I simply looked at each other and politely changed the conversation. While we spoke about the church bake sale, a Bible study class, and other topics from the church, my mind kept spinning with thoughts of Joseph.

After a few hours, we sent the good Reverend Simmons on his way. Ruth and I quietly collected the various dirty dishes in our kitchen and began to stack them on the marble counter top by the sink. Ruth washed, I dried, and then we began to talk about our visitor.

"He has quite a healthy appetite," Ruth stated.

"Always a good eater," I agreed.

"I wonder if that's a reflection on our cooking?" Ruth asked.

"Or a reflection on the size of his stomach," I laughed.

"Perhaps," Ruth replied.

We grew quiet while I washed and Ruth dried the dishes. When I finished with the last of the utensils, I dried my hands, leaned back on the counter, and looked Ruth square in the eye.

"You know, sister, I think we should talk to Miles," I stated.

"Why?" Ruth asked.

"He's the only member of the family we haven't spoken with. He really is the one person who can help us get to the root of our questions," I answered. "The only issue is how do we get to Miles?"

CHAPTER EIGHTEEN: MONEY AND MOTIVE

Miles Campbell was president of one of the oldest banks in the city, Washington National Bank. It was a position he'd held for many years. Stability was the nature of banking and, in my opinion, it's what gave Miles job security as the bank's president.

One byproduct of his position came in the form of all the networking Miles did with other bankers, investors, and politicians. Whether it was small talk over drinks, chatting between rounds of golf, or enjoying lunch with a client, Miles was intimately familiar with how Washington money flowed. He knew what was in the pockets of most senators and representatives, and he also knew how the money got there. He even knew what groups were donating to what legislature for re-election or for influence over a bill. In a town built on power, it was always difficult for the average person to look into the political tea leaves and make a judgment about the motives behind why a particular senator or representative was voting a certain way. Not so for Miles Campbell.

Complimenting the financial insights of Miles were the social connections of Natalie. Together they were always in demand at parties to clear the muddy political waters for anyone who cared to listen to them. However, the matter of their son's death had become the hot topic of gossip in Washington, which led them both to become strangely silent at social events.

This was the challenge the day that Ruth and I stepped through the front door of Washington National

Bank. Ruth and I knew it would be difficult to get Miles to speak about his son's death. Because of his position with the bank, I also knew it also would be difficult for us to even gain access to him. I'm quite certain that running a bank makes for a busy schedule. In fact, in my past conversations with Natalie, she often remarked about how busy Miles was.

So the challenge for Ruth and me was quite clear as we stood in the pristine marble lobby of the bank. How would we be able to interrupt the busy schedule of a president of a bank? I knew it would require us to do something dramatic to warrant any employee to call Miles. It had to be something so important that it would warrant him to leave his office to come and acknowledge us. The predicament caused me to think of something my mother would say:

"If you want to marry a banker, money is what always gets their attention."

Despite being dead for many years, our mother's advice would prove most helpful to us in this matter.

When we walked around the bank, the marble floors glistened, thanks in part to a grand chandelier that hung from above. Black leather chairs were scattered around the lobby, as were desks where bank officials sat and worked. A set of steps, at the far end of the lobby, led to a second floor where I guessed offices were located. Ruth and I approached a desk where a clean-cut young man stood up and grinned at us.

"May I help you, ladies?" he asked, tucking his hands behind his back.

"Yes," Ruth nodded and she reached into her handbag and pulled out her checkbook.

"We're here to inquire about your certificates of deposit. The rates you have are very nice which is why we're interested in opening an account."

"We do pride ourselves in offering the best rates in town," the young man smiled and he gestured to a couple of black leather chairs across from his desk. Ruth and I quickly sat down and watched him grab a pen and some papers.

"What is your name, dear?" I asked.

"Mitch Mallard," he replied. "And you are?"

"Charlotte and Ruth Dupree," I replied.

"Nice to meet you," he said, while scribbling on some paper.

"Well, Mitch," I began, "as I said, my sister and I would like to open a CD account. What is the duration that you offer a CD to come to maturity?"

"We have different CD's for different rates," Mitch explained, putting his pen down and making direct eye contact with us for the first time. "Of course, the longer you ladies can keep your money in, the better your rate of return will be."

"I see," I nodded and smiled at Ruth. "Of course, at our age we might be rolling the dice with a one year CD. How about six months? Would that sound good to you, Ruth?"

"Six months sounds delightful," Ruth grinned.

"Very good," I said. "Six months it is then, Mitch."

"That sounds like a good number to me." Mitch nodded and he picked up his pen again and began to write down more information on the documents he had neatly arranged on his desk. "Now, of course, to open an account here, you ladies will need a minimum deposit of one thousand dollars. Are you ladies prepared to do that amount?"

"We were actually thinking of a different amount," I smiled.

"Well," Mitch sighed, "one thousand would be the minimum. How much would you two nice ladies be able to scrape together?"

"Two million dollars," I stated.

Mitch dropped his pen. His face grew bright red and he quickly picked it up.

"Are you okay?" Ruth asked. "You're looking a little…warm."

"I…I'm sorry," Mitch said and he shook his head and leaned back in his chair. "You surprised me. I just didn't expect you two nice ladies to have—say—that…amount."

"Well," I replied, "mother and father left us a good bit of money. Over the years, we've made some good investments so…we have enough to throw around."

"And enough for our Tums," Ruth giggled.

"I'm going to have to call someone about this amount," Mitch stammered while he reached for the phone.

"If Mr. Campbell is here," I said, pointing across the desk, "he knows us. Tell him to come down. We'd love to have a moment with him."

"Yes," Mitch agreed before picking up a phone and nervously pressing some buttons.

A few minutes later, a familiar face appeared from a side door in the lobby. It was Miles Campbell. His white hair was easy to spot. Tall and lean he moved through the lobby, offering a polite smile to customers. When he made eye contact with us, he waved Ruth and me over to a carpeted area next to the lobby. He gestured to some leather chairs fixed around a small oak desk where the three of us sat. Again, he offered the same polite smile, which I could tell was hard for him to muster.

"Good morning, Dupree sisters," he said in a tone of voice that was more professional than friendly. Miles had two papers that he laid flat on the desk before us. Then he cleared his throat, glanced at both of us once and pointed at the paper.

"It's good to see you, Miles," I stated.

"Two million dollars for six month?" Miles replied and he shook his head with a little grin riding his lips. "Ruth and Charlotte, I've buried myself in paperwork this week. Kept myself in my office most of the time. You're the only customers I've spoken to since the funeral…because what you're doing doesn't make sense."

"We're honored," Ruth smiled.

"It's not an honor to be reckless with your money," Miles scolded. "The beauty of being your age is that you two should enjoy every day. Take every trip. Spend your money on the things you want. Tying up funds like this for six months for a small interest rate in return just doesn't make sense to me."

Miles grew silent and he stared across the table at us, tapping one finger on one of the documents. I wasn't sure if he wanted us to say something else or not.

"Miles, I …" Ruth began to say.

"Normally," Miles interrupted, "I would have other people here to counsel you ladies on what you're doing, but since we've known each other for so long I thought it would mean more coming from me. This is not a good idea, ladies."

"Miles," I smiled. "You know we've been members of this bank for a long time. You know how many millions of dollars we have in here."

"True," Miles replied. "I'm ten years younger than you and I'm already at the age where I wouldn't take six months for granted. Life can change rather quickly…which is another reason not to tie up your money this way."

"Your concern is well founded…given everything that's happened the last few weeks," I said, sensing an opening to turn the conversation away from us and towards Joseph.

"Yes," Ruth said. "That tragic situation with your son. Oh, Miles, we really are so sorry to hear about that. Joseph was such a sweet boy when he was younger."

"He was a good boy," Miles replied, again his eyes darting down to the documents on the desk. "I've...I've had a lot of time to think since Joseph's death and I've come to the conclusion that life shouldn't rush our children into being adults. Childhood is like a cocoon. Natalie and I...we're more aware of that now. I'm just thankful I can come to work and put that pain out of my mind for a few hours a day."

"Grace said you'd made some tough decisions regarding Joseph," Ruth said. "Drug addiction is a terrible thing."

I glanced at Ruth. I was a bit surprised that she actually made the statement, but Ruth was always the one who spoke her mind and never sugar-coated any words.

"Let me talk about these forms," Miles stammered and he tapped his hands on the two pieces of paper. "These forms are what you would need to sign if you want your money deposited. I don't think it would be a very wise move, ladies, but it's your money."

"Miles," I began. "May I ask one question about Joseph?"

Miles closed his eyes and his hands slowly slipped off the documents. He sat back in his seat and looked at us.

"The day he left the house...did you ever see Joseph again?" I asked.

"No," he quickly replied and his eyes narrowed the way a father's eyes do before a lecture. "It was a decision I had to stand firm on, ladies. He was a man and he'd made his choices, as did I. None of us thought it would end this way."

"Ruth and I donated money to the shelter that was helping Joseph," I began. "The shelter is run by a very nice man named Gus Munchack. He gave Joseph a bed to sleep on and food to eat. He could tell you more about Joseph's last days staying there."

"No," Miles replied and he blinked a few times, as if processing what we'd just told him. "Tell this man I said thank you for taking care of my son, but…I can't….I….I won't go there. I have enough trouble walking by those steps at our church."

With those words, Miles carefully slid a pen across the desk to us. He leaned back in his chair and took a deep breath. He rubbed his eyes with both hands then stood up.

"If you sign these forms…give them to Mitch and I'll have the funds transferred later today," he stated. "Good day, ladies."

With those words, Miles stood up. He didn't smile or say a word. Looking at him, the expression on his face reminded me of the expression I saw at the cemetery. A sad expression that looked more natural on his face than a smile. I kept my eye on Miles as he quietly retreated to a door to the side of the lobby, where I guessed his office was located. I turned back to Ruth, who was looking right at me. Neither one of us knew what to say.

"Well…that was awkward," Ruth observed.

"What you said didn't help," I replied.

"It was necessary," Ruth stated. "This was probably our only time to talk to Miles. I wanted to lay everything out so he knew what we knew."

"Agreed," I replied. "You're always too direct, sister, but in this case I think you were right to say what you did."

"He's clearly in pain," Ruth stated. "Getting him to speak on the matter was difficult."

"It will always be difficult," I said and I reached over and picked up the documents Miles had given us. "He's one reason why Joseph is dead. He knows it, which is why he's burying his guilt and grief in his job."

"I believe what he said about not seeing his son after he sent him away," Ruth observed.

"I believe him too," I nodded. "Grief has left him raw and honest."

"I think we're done here, sister," Ruth said.

I tore the papers in half and stood up.

"Yes," Ruth agreed and she gestured at the papers on the desk. "This was a good idea. You were right, Charlotte. Luring Miles out with a good deal of money was a brilliant stroke. It was like…waving a piece of meat in front of a lion."

"Agreed," I answered. "So we know that Miles wasn't having a change of heart and giving Joseph money for things."

"And Natalie?" Ruth asked.

"I know Natalie can be tough, but I don't think she would have gone against Miles," I replied. "Not on a matter this serious. She knew drugs would kill Joseph, so it just doesn't make sense to suspect her of giving him money."

"Then who?" Ruth asked.

"That does seem to be the question of the day," I smiled.

As we left the bank, rain was just starting to drop on the city. I quickly popped open my umbrella. Ruth and I huddled under it while we waited for a taxi to come by. This particular spring shower didn't feel like a warm one to me. In fact, the rain felt raw and cool and for a brief moment it felt like I was back at the cemetery, burying Joseph and mourning his death. It was the kind of feeling that only gets magnified by dark days like this.

CHAPTER NINETEEN: TIME TO PAUSE

Charlotte sat back in her chair. Her mind pulled itself back from the memories that were filling her head. She smacked her lips together and sensed her mouth was dry from all the talking she'd been doing. She looked at her guest. Mr. Cabbott stared back at her from the couch. The expression on his face told her he was curious why she'd stopped talking. Ruth glanced at Charlotte and then back to Mr. Cabbott before turning back to Charlotte again.

"Is there something wrong, sister?" Ruth finally asked. "Did you lose your train of thought? I know sometimes it leaves the station without telling me."

"No," Charlotte replied. "I just realized that we may have been giving a false impression of ourselves to our guest."

"How so?" Ruth asked.

Mr. Cabbott put his pen down on his notepad.

"Miss Dupree," Neil said, checking his watch. "I hope you're not making all this up. I've been here for a good many hours, and I've got pages of notes. Please don't tell me you're making up some of the facts. Please tell me you've been honest and you have an ending."

"No, I'm not making this up," Charlotte quickly responded. "Everything I've said is on the up and up. I was actually sitting here thinking about how I've portrayed myself and my sister. With everything I've said you might believe that my sister and I only leave the house for social engagements like luncheons, banquets, high society teas, and other affairs that require us to dress to the hilt. In fact, there's one place that Ruth and I enjoy going to that doesn't require us to put on fancy clothes, makeup, or even our best shoes."

"A spa?" Mr. Cabbott guessed.

"No," Charlotte answered with a wide grin. "At our age, no one wants to see us strolling around a spa in nothing but a robe."

"Heavens no," Ruth giggled.

"No, Mr. Cabbott, we enjoy going to the zoo to relax," Charlotte stated.

"The zoo?" Mr. Cabbott asked, and for the first time all day he didn't write down what Charlotte told him.

"Oh, yes," Ruth replied, sitting up in her seat. "Charlotte and I do enjoy a stroll through the zoo. We quite like watching the pandas the best."

"They are very playful." Charlotte nodded. "Sometimes watching playful behavior helps me to relax. When I relax, my mind becomes more active in thinking of ways to do things."

"Have you been to the zoo, Mr. Cabbott?" Ruth asked.

"Call me Neil," he responded. "No…I haven't really had any spare time to go…with work and all."

"It really is quite a treat," Ruth replied.

"I read somewhere," Charlotte began, "that President Benjamin Harrison not only approved of the chosen site, but he also reviewed the price for the land before signing legislation to pay for it. At 166 acres, who could blame him for reviewing the price."

"Those fuzzy pandas are just so adorable," Ruth giggled. "If we're having a tough time with things, or a down day, Charlotte and I go to the zoo and those pandas always put a smile on our faces. You must take the time to go."

"I'll try to remember that," Mr. Cabbott smiled politely while writing down his promise. "So after you met with Miles Campbell…you two went to the zoo?"

"The next day was warm and sunny and we needed a place to think," Charlotte recalled. "You see, Ruth and I felt like we weren't getting anywhere with our investigation. While we learned a lot of things, we still didn't know the truth behind what had happened to poor little Jo-Jo Campbell, which is what we wanted to know."

"And it was while we were at the zoo," Ruth recalled, "that we had a discussion about the family. That's when we had our big break."

"While at the zoo?" Neil asked, before writing more notes.

"Let me explain," Charlotte began.

She took a deep breath, let the memories of the previous weeks fill her head again, and then took a sip of water to quench her dry mouth before beginning to share what she recalled in resolving the death of Joseph Campbell.

CHAPTER TWENTY: THE INDULGENCE OF PANDAS

Going to the National Zoo in Washington always brings back good memories for Ruth and me. Ever since we were young girls, we've always enjoyed going to the zoo with our parents. Thanks to President Harrison, the National Zoo has been an enduring legacy for generations of tourists and residents.

Whenever Ruth and I go to the zoo, it brings out the child in both of us. We giggle and laugh at some of the animals. If it's a nice day, Ruth and I will spend a few hours walking around and enjoying the animals. On a sun-drenched day, when the temperature is just right, I can't think of any place better to go. While we enjoy all the animals on display, there's one particular creature that I simply must make a point of seeing.

A day at the zoo is not complete until I've persuaded my sister to follow me to the panda bear habitat. While the lions, monkeys, and giraffes are all well and good, there is something about panda bears that I find simply irresistible. In a world where everyone is in a hurry, I take great pleasure in watching the leisurely way pandas walk, eat and simply enjoy their surroundings. They also can melt my heart when I watch them sleep. Yet, what always makes me laugh is when I see a panda eating. The way a panda sits, with its round belly nearly touching the ground, is an indication to me that it's well fed. Yet, when I watch a panda bear eat, the pleasure it takes in devouring whatever food it is given makes me laugh. This is especially true when it eats bamboo. One morning when Ruth and I were there, we sat on our favorite bench and watched a panda bear chew away on one bamboo stick after another. The sight simply made me laugh so hard my face must have turned three shades of red.

"Isn't he a hungry fellow?" I asked in between my giggles.

"Apparently," Ruth chimed in with a more composed tone in her voice.

"How a simple act like eating can bring so much joy to one animal is a secret that we humans could learn from," I observed.

"Chocolate has the same effect on me," Ruth pointed out.

I looked at her and we both laughed at her comment.

"Simple pleasures," I sighed. "Life is full of them. While I enjoy chocolate, a good nap is one of my simple pleasures. When I sit down and close my eyes on a sunny afternoon, I know there are many things to do, but sneaking in that nap just makes me feel better."

"Eating and sleeping," Ruth observed. "If those are our guilty pleasures, we certainly are not all that exciting, are we, sister? You know how the famous people take pleasure in more racy things like affairs, alcohol or drugs. For us, it's chocolate and napping."

"So true, sister," I laughed. "At least our habits don't require a nasty bill from a lawyer or a chemical dependency center."

"So true," Ruth added. "There are so many things that we take for granted that can be good pleasures to indulge in. I'd suppose we would come to appreciate those simple pleasures more if they were taken from us."

"I'm quite certain Joseph Campbell felt that way when he was homeless," I sighed. "When you're living in a homeless shelter, and you only have a bed and three square meals, I'd imagine you'd find pleasures in those simple things."

"Yes," Ruth replied. "Little Jo-Jo was very lucky that he had someone like Gus Munchack to help him."

"Indeed," I said. "Living on the streets, Joseph was quite lucky to have a place to go for some sleep, and meals to eat."

"I think Miles should thank Gus for what he did for Joseph," Ruth said.

"Miles can be stubborn that way," I remarked and my words were followed by my head shaking from side to side. "Sometimes Miles is proud to a fault."

"He does have a stubborn streak," Ruth said. "Perhaps someone else from the family would be willing to go with us to see Gus and thank him. I think it would be proper for someone from the family to acknowledge Gus. It might also help the family to heal if someone were to go there and look at the shelter and see where Joseph spent the final days of his life."

"Miles and Natalie are too broken up," Ruth stated. "I mean, Miles pretty much waved off the idea when I brought it up at the bank."

"Then lets call the children," I suggested. "Grace, Tom or Ethan. Maybe they would all like to come with us to see the shelter and meet Gus."

"It certainly wouldn't hurt to ask," I agreed. "It may even help to give some closure."

Together we stayed a bit longer. We watched the panda bear finish his snack, then stood up and strolled around a bit more. The creatures appeared content. The visitors were happy. The day was sunny and warm. Ruth and I laughed some more and a feeling of our youthfulness spilled over us as we smiled and pointed at the animals on display for a little while longer.

CHAPTER TWENTY-ONE: SOUP AND SOLUTIONS

One evening, Ruth and I were sitting in the kitchen enjoying a lovely dinner of soup and crackers. While soup doesn't sound like a meal to most people, this particular brand is quite filling for us. Not far from our house is a small corner deli that sells, in my opinion, the best broccoli and cheddar soup in town. It is thick and tasty and makes for a satisfying meal for both of us.

While we enjoyed our soup, the dinner conversation eventually led to our lack of progress in learning more about Joseph Campbell's death. We still didn't know who was giving him clean needles and we weren't any closer to figuring out how he was able to buy drugs. We felt like we'd spoken to everyone involved. In short, we were stumped by the whole situation.

"Hopeless," Ruth sighed while she blew into her bowl. "We've talked to every member of the family and we still don't know what happened to Little Jo-Jo."

"Agreed," I sighed, before taking my first bite of soup. "We've talked to Reverend Simmons, all the members of the Campbell family and Gus Munchack. While I hate to say it, perhaps we've gone as far as we can with this matter, Ruth. Is it possible that we won't ever have these questions answered?"

"You're giving up?" Ruth asked.

"No…merely stating my frustration," I replied.

With those words, I looked down at the thin veils of steam spinning up from my bowl. The aroma was warm and intoxicating and I quickly grabbed my spoon and began to stir my broccoli and cheddar soup.

"I just think we've learned as much as we can from the people we talked to…and we've run out of people to meet with to learn the truth about why he died," I pointed out.

"You're assuming that the people we spoke with are being honest with us, sister," Ruth added.

"You think someone is lying?" I asked and then blew into my bowl in another futile attempt to cool my soup.

"There are many parts of this town that run on lies and deception," Ruth explained. "Maybe I've been breathing too much of the political air, but I just don't trust what people tell me anymore."

When she finished her statement, we scooped up some soup, blew on our respective spoons and savored the first bites of our dinner. The taste danced on my tongue and I couldn't help but smile.

"Well, that's quite a cynical point of view, Ruth," I finally replied. "These aren't politicians were talking about. This is a good family that we've known for many years. We've worshipped with them and watched their children grow into adults. I think we are the best of acquaintances with the Campbells. To assume one of them is lying is….thinking the worst."

"You may be right, Charlotte," Ruth mumbled, before taking another bite of soup. "We all have secrets to hide. Some of us have more than others. I don't think the Campbells are any different than some of the politicians in Washington. They have private matters just like a senator or a representative and they'll be very careful to guard those secrets."

"Point taken," I nodded, before slipping another spoonful of soup in my mouth.

"Why don't we talk to Grace again?" Ruth suggested before crumbling some crackers into her soup. "She told us she visited with Joseph a few times. She was the only one of the family to have contact with him. Maybe she could tell us if she thought Joseph had any friends at that shelter."

"Grace doesn't know anything," I mumbled without even thinking. My heart had quickly dictated my response to this suggestion. I shook my head when I thought of Grace. "I don't want to bother her."

"Why not?" Ruth asked. "She already said she was seeing Joseph at church. It's not like we're suspecting her of giving him clean needles."

"Because I know Grace!" I snapped and I could feel my voice grow a little louder out of frustration with what Ruth was implying.

"Charlotte?" Ruth asked. "Why are you raising your voice?"

"Grace is in mourning. Her brother is dead and she's trying to get over that. I just think we need to respect that now," I answered in a softer tone of voice.

I took another sip of my soup and didn't say any more on the matter. Ruth quietly went back to eating her soup. I always thought of Grace as the daughter I'd never had. Our bond had been a good one for a long time. I trusted what Grace said to be the truth and what Ruth was saying challenged that long held belief.

"We've spoken to everyone else. Grace is the only one who communicated with Joseph. It just makes sense to talk to her some more," Ruth finally remarked.

I took a deep breath and quietly nodded at my sister's sound reasoning. I scooped up some more soup, slipped it in my mouth and thought about what Ruth was saying. Most of the time, my sister acts out of emotion, but in this case her thinking was more rational than mine.

"I just...I feel like we've bothered Grace enough with this matter," I sighed and I grabbed a glass and took a sip of water. "We spoke to her at the funeral. We spoke to her again in church. If we meet with her for a third time...I'd feel like we were just dragging her back through this muddy situation again. She's young and newly married and should be enjoying this time in her life."

"But she might be able to help us," Ruth pressed.

"Grace is such a sweet girl," I sighed. "I know she wouldn't mind talking to us, but I'm quite certain she's trying to focus on more pleasant things. No one likes being pulled through the muck of mourning for a loved one."

"Well, then, sister, we need to put a positive spin on this. We need to extend an invitation and we need to make our invitation sound as pleasant and happy as possible for Grace to accept," Ruth suggested.

"What are you thinking?" I asked.

"Maybe you should offer to take her to lunch or dinner," Ruth said and she smiled at her suggestion. "It's clear to me you're a good dinner companion. Besides, Grace likes your company. Tell Grace you want to take her out to talk about all the things she's has been doing with her job and her marriage."

"Perhaps lunch would better fit with her schedule," I replied. "She wouldn't want to leave her husband to dine with me."

"Why not invite them both?" Ruth asked, sitting up a little straighter. "Tell her you'd like to meet him. Take them both out for dinner as a belated wedding gift. It certainly would be more fun and casual if Grace brought her husband to meet you."

"That is a wonderful idea," I grinned.

Grace quietly nodded and together we resumed eating our soup.

"You know, sister," I said while blowing on another spoonful of soup, "there are times in life when I think I can predict everything you'll say or do….and then there are times when you surprise me."

"I've kept you on your toes since I was six…and I don't intend to stop now," Ruth laughed.

CHAPTER TWENTY TWO: DINNER

A few days later, I found myself seated at a classic restaurant in downtown Washington. *Old Ebbitt Grill* has been a historic landmark in Washington for as long as I can remember. It was the restaurant Grace chose because she thought I would like it. The reasoning behind her choice was typical of Grace—to think of someone else rather than herself. It was a quality she'd possessed since she was a child. It was also a quality that I thought might have led her to provide a good deal of support for Joseph.

Seated around a small rectangular table covered by a white tablecloth, Grace and I waited for her husband to arrive from work. A small lamp on the table cast a dim light between us as we talked about her job, her husband and her wedding. It was the kind of delightful chit-chat that reminded me of how wonderful youth can be. Listening to Grace speak about her hopes, her dreams, and her goals for the future was a refreshing change of pace from the conversations I usually endured with my contemporaries. When one reaches a certain age, instead of hopes and dreams, conversations tend to focus on mutual friends who've died and mutual aches and pains.

"You know," I told Grace as she glanced around the room, "they say that Grover Cleveland, Teddy Roosevelt and Warren Harding came here for a stiff drink when they were president. If I were president...I think I'd need more than *one* stiff drink!"

"I knew this place was old...I just didn't know it was *that* old." Grace smiled and her eyes lingered on the people around us. "I like to come here because it's close to work and I like the food. I didn't know the history all that much. You always know a lot of interesting details about this town, Miss Dupree."

"Growing up here helps," I smiled.

Suddenly a strange sound like a cowbell could be heard. For a second I thought a cow had managed to enter the restaurant. Then I saw Grace quickly turn in her chair, reach into her purse and pull out her phone. She poked at the screen with one finger, then read something that caused her to shake her head.

"Tripp is hung up at the office," Grace sighed, slipping the phone back into her purse.

"Who?" I asked.

"Tripp is my husband," she replied. "He told me what to order for him. He'll be a little late…but he promises he'll be here. I told him I'd order for him. I also told him all about you, Miss Dupree. He can't wait to meet you."

"Tripp is lucky to be married to you," I grinned.

Grace smiled and she looked at me in a way that, for a few seconds, resembled a newlywed in love and not a sister in mourning.

"So where did you two meet?" I asked.

"A pub!" Grace laughed for the first time since we'd entered the restaurant. "I know it doesn't sound like the most romantic place. Tripp was helping a buddy of his with a place called Brew'd Pub just outside of Washington. It's a beautiful old tavern with lovely hardwood floors and delicious food. I was in college, serving an internship for a brokerage firm, and I'd go to Brew'd Pub for lunch. Tripp was still in college and tending bar part-time at the pub. He served me a pastrami on rye and we started talking. Before I knew it…I didn't want to stop talking to him."

"Oh, Grace, I'm so happy for you," I grinned and I reached across the table and patted her on the hand. "It must be nice to find someone to love and spend the rest of your life with."

"I'm happy," Grace grinned, then she straightened up in her seat and cleared her throat. "So how about you, Miss Dupree? How are you doing?"

"Ruth and I still keep busy," I said, raising my voice to compensate for some laughter coming from the bar. "We still attend the important events of the social season. Sometimes I have to look in the mirror to remind myself of my age. I still feel like the same person from twenty years ago. However, the mirror in my bathroom has a different opinion."

"Well….despite your mirror…I still think you look great," Grace smiled. "I also think it's nice that you and your sister are still so active. Do you two still own season tickets to the Washington Redskins?"

"We gave those up years ago," I laughed. "They were a terrible football team and we just stopped going. We're still fans, though. We watch them play every Sunday…and we still yell at the TV with the same passion that our father had."

Grace looked at me and nodded with a grin on her face. She reached for a menu and began to study it. I did the same. A few feet away from us I could hear voices at the bar. Out of the corner of my eye I could see young professionals gathered at the bar, tipping back drinks and chatting to each other. It brought back memories of my days on the Hill, going for drinks after work with colleagues from the House to reflect on the latest legislation our boss was supporting or shooting down. Working for a representative right out of high school, I had such passion for politics back in those days. Listening to the voices of the young people hanging out at the bar, the words I heard sounded vaguely familiar.

"Tripp enjoys the steak here," Grace said.

"What?" I asked, trying to regain my focus.

"I said Tripp likes the steak here," she mentioned. "I prefer the pork."

"Have you ever tried the glazed meatloaf?" I asked.

"No," Grace replied, still studying the menu.

"Then meatloaf it is," I replied.

With that decision made, we put our menus to the side and waited for someone to come and take our orders. While we waited, I could sense the silence building between us. I thought that maybe this was the right time to get my questions out of the way so the majority of the evening could be spent talking about happier topics.

"Grace," I began. "I don't mean to pry…but how are you doing? It's been a harrowing few weeks for you and your family. How are you coping?"

Grace's dark eyes shifted down to the table and her expression changed from festive to sullen in less than a second.

"I try to keep busy," she mumbled and those sad eyes that Grace had since childhood turned up and looked right at me. "It's like…in my mind he isn't gone. I was always so busy with work and coming home to Tripp that…I had to make the time to find Joey. He never called me. I always had to make the effort to find him."

"And how did you do that?" I asked.

"Ethan kept in touch with Joey," Grace explained. "He was sort of our go between. Ethan would tell Joey when I wanted to see him. I'd bring him some food I knew he liked. When it got colder I gave Joey a pair of gloves, too."

"Any money?" I asked.

"No," Grace replied. "I didn't know what he'd use it for. My husband had a friend on drugs. Tripp suggested I not give Joey money because he'd be tempted to buy more drugs. Church and the shelter were the two places I'd go to meet him. If it weren't for Ethan's help, I don't think I could have ever found Joey. He never came over to visit or call me. So like I said…I know he's dead but…part of me feels like he's still out there walking the streets."

"When you talked to him," I began and I paused for a moment to get my words straight before speaking. "Did Joseph ever mention if he had any friends at the shelter? Any people he kept company with?"

"Not that I know of," Grace replied.

"When you saw him…were there any other people around him? Any faces that you'd remember seeing over and over again?" I asked.

Grace sat back in her seat and again her eyes glanced down on the table like her memories had tumbled out onto her placemat.

"I don't remember seeing anyone with Joey," Grace answered in a soft voice. "He was always alone when we met. What I do remember is how awful he smelled. One time I remember thinking that no one would want to get near him because he hadn't taken a bath in weeks."

"Yes," Charlotte said. "I'd suppose the shelter where Joseph stayed was more concerned with food and rest than with his cleanliness. He was lucky to have a place to go."

Grace sighed and I could see her looking beyond me. Looking at the bar behind me. In thinking back on it, I'd suppose she was looking at the young people drinking, talking politics and having fun recounting the events of the day. She stared at the carefree scene filled with people her own age and I'm quite certain she wanted to be there rather than talking to me about Joseph.

"I told my parents I don't want to go back to our church again," Grace finally said. "I grew up at St. Johns but…with what happened to Joey on the steps…I just don't want to go there anymore."

"I can't say that I blame you," I sighed with a nod. "I still have questions about what happened there. I know the police think it was a robbery, but I doubt it. I keep thinking about the clean needles he had. He was staying in a shelter that wouldn't allow drugs inside. Any person addicted to drugs wouldn't be giving away clean needles. They'd be using them. So where were those needles coming from? Were you giving them to him?"

"No!" Grace quickly answered and her eyebrows dropped down and her face grew flushed. "Why would you ask me that?"

"Because I want to know what happened to your brother," I said with a tone that was respectful but direct.

I remember watching Grace wipe her eyes with the back of her hand and she began to blink very quickly.

"The answer isn't going to bring him back…so I really don't care," she whispered and she wiped her eyes again and smiled. "Can we talk about something else?"

"Of course," I smiled.

It seemed to me I was digging for something that wasn't there. In my attempt to get to the truth I was causing some real pain for Grace, and it wasn't what I'd intended to do.

Finally, the waitress came and took our order. Grace excused herself and returned from the bar with a drink. A few minutes later Tripp finally arrived and his smile, energy and laughter changed the mood at our table. I noticed how just the sight of her husband caused Grace's demeanor to turn for the better.

As the evening commenced, I enjoyed my meatloaf from start to finish. I also enjoyed the company of a young couple in love. Listening to them giggle at each other, smile after every story, and speak about their plans for the future was quite invigorating. By dessert it was clear to me that Grace had found a good man, which in Washington can sometimes be a challenge. It was a challenge that Ruth and I were never able to resolve as confirmed bachelorettes.

Soon I found myself sitting in a cab, riding home, reflecting on my evening. What I'd learned from Grace was that her brother was close to no one. Perhaps he simply didn't trust the people in the shelter. Maybe he didn't trust anyone, which is probably the nature of a person who is homeless and grappling with a drug problem. Whatever the reason, Joseph simply had no one close to him once his family abandoned him. Grace also seemed genuinely upset when I asked her about the needles.

Driving by the U.S. Capitol, I couldn't help but marvel at how lovely the dome looked. Though I'd seen it a thousand times, it still took my breath away when cast against a lavender sky at sunset. It got me thinking about the building and my years working there. Men and women have worked there for many years making laws that affect people from the east coast to the west coast and everywhere in between. Having worked for a representative, I can understand how one can support or lobby against legislation based on the face attached to the bill and not on the millions of people it will affect. It's easy to lose sight of people when you can't see them or hear from them. That's why I was proud of Grace. Even though Joseph was roaming the streets, and didn't make the effort to contact her, Grace didn't want to forget about him. However, I was surprised to learn that Ethan also was keeping contact with Joseph. It's a detail he'd failed to mention to me. I was curious as to why.

CHAPTER TWENTY-THREE: EXTENDING INVITATIONS

A college professor and an art gallery curator have busy schedules. There was never a doubt in my mind about that. Yet, I felt it imperative to call both Thomas and Ethan to put forth an invitation to have them meet Gus Munchack.

We first called Thomas, who was quite taken with the idea of thanking the man who had been watching over his little brother. However, Thomas explained that he was coming up on the end of the spring semester. He was quite busy taking in meetings with students and could only go with us in a few weeks. While he sounded very interested in going to Holy Redeemer Shelter, he also knew his responsibilities at work came first. In the end, he agreed to go with us at a later date. Thomas always had that practical nature, even as a boy. Work came first and we agreed to his request.

Ethan was a different matter. We had a lengthy conversation with him about Holy Redeemer Shelter. When I brought up the idea, Ethan quickly agreed to meet us. He asked us the name of the man we were going to meet and sounded like he was excited to thank him. Unlike Thomas, Ethan seemed to have more flexibility in his schedule. I was surprised at how uncomplicated it was for him to commit to our invitation.

A few days later, Ethan agreed to meet with Ruth and me at St. John's Church. Together we stood and talked for a good bit about the gallery opening. When the conversation waned we began to walk the familiar route to Holy Redeemer Shelter. The sun was bright and I could actually hear a robin chirping from on top of a building. It was a pleasant spring day that made seeing a robin all the more heartwarming to me.

"You're a good brother for doing this," I heard Ruth tell Ethan.

"It's the least I can do," Ethan replied. "Like you said, someone from the family *should* thank this Munchack guy for what he did for Joey. I thought about it and I'd like to donate some money to his shelter, too. If there are more people in Joey's situation I want to help them."

"A donation is a nice idea," Ruth said.

"From what Gus told us, he provides for a good many people. Not just men…but women and children. I'm certain any donation you give would be greatly appreciated," I explained.

The walk to the shelter was a pleasant one. Unlike Grace, Ethan seemed to be coping well with his brother's death. I couldn't wait to arrive at the shelter to see Ethan's face when he met Gus. I also couldn't wait to see Gus's reaction to the news about the donation.

When we arrived at the shelter, I knocked on the door and was surprised to see it open as soon as I stopped. Gus Munchack appeared in the doorway, his face looking as tired and sweated as it had the last time I'd seen him.

"Ladies," he grunted and his chiseled expression formed a brief smile. "What brings you back here?"

"Gus," I began, "I wanted to introduce you to a friend."

I gestured to Ethan and before I could say another word, I watched Gus turn his eyes to Ethan. For me, it was one of those moments that happened in slow motion. I saw Gus's eyes go from calm to narrow and I watched his face transform into what I could only describe as looking like an angry dog.

"Get *him* out of here!" Gus snapped. He pointed at me and Ruth and his voice grew louder and sharper. "I told you two not to go looking for drug dealers! I warned you! Why in the hell would you bring him around here? You know I don't allow drug dealers near this shelter!"

Without warning, he made a fist, stepped forward and punched Ethan right in the face.

"Gus!" I heard Ruth shout.

I was stunned. I stood there with my mouth hanging open as I watched Ethan drop to the ground like a sack of potatoes. I looked at Gus and my anger boiled.

"Stop!" I finally yelled, stepping between Gus and Ethan. "Stop it, Gus! What are you doing?"

"Drug dealers are like rats. Can't show them any kindness," Gus grunted and he finally stepped back from Ethan, who was curled up on the street. "That scum ain't nothing but trouble!"

I looked at Ethan and the way he was holding his face reminded me of the one time I saw him as a boy get into a tussle with another boy after church before getting punched. Ruth helped Ethan to his feet and he stepped behind Ruth and myself for protection from Gus. I turned to Gus and he simply stood there shaking his head. He was clearly having trouble getting hold of his temper.

"Mr. Munchack!" Ruth snapped. "This is Ethan Campbell. This is Joseph Campbell's brother. We brought him here to thank you for what you were doing for Joseph...not to punch him in the nose!"

"Brother?" Gus yelled and he looked at Ethan and his eyes narrowed. "Let me tell you something. I got security cameras all around the outside of this building. I've seen this guy with Joseph in the alley more than once. They didn't know I was watching but I was. I saw this guy passing off money to Joseph. Money that Joseph was using for drugs. One time, I even saw this guy give his brother some needles. I checked Joe for drugs every night before I let him spend the night. He never had any drugs on him, but I could tell he was doing drugs. So, ladies, I don't really care if this *is* Joe's brother. This guy is nothing more than a drug dealer to me. He kept Joe hooked on the stuff. Now get him out!"

Well, of course, Ruth and I were shocked at what we were being told. Our house wasn't all that far away from the shelter so we did as Gus requested before he hit Ethan again. Ruth took some tissues from her purse and instructed Ethan on how to hold it to his nose to stop the bleeding. Ethan was quick to follow Ruth's direction, holding the tissue on his nose at just the right place to slow down the blood. I took Ethan by the hand and the three of us walked a few blocks to our home.

As we walked, I couldn't help but notice the strange looks being directed at Ruth and myself from people we passed along the way. Some of the expressions told me they were wondering if two little old ladies had actually beaten up this strapping young man.

When we returned to the house, we took Ethan into the kitchen where we washed the blood off his face and his hands as best we could. While we cleaned him up, Ethan would whimper like a boy. He talked about the pain he was in and we suggested putting an ice pack on his nose. It had really swelled up pretty quickly and Ethan feared it was broken.

After a few minutes, Ethan began to feel a little better. The bleeding stopped and I gave him some aspirin for the pain. Ruth suggested we move into the sitting room for more comfortable furniture to sit on.

Ethan continued to whimper like a schoolboy and we did our best to make him comfortable on the couch.

Once he was lying down, with ice on his nose, Ruth and I simply sat on a couple of chairs across from him and watched Ethan as he touched his nose every so often and winced at the pain.

"Do you think it's broken?" he finally asked, turning to us the way a child does for reassurance. "Does it look like it's broken?"

"Your nose appears to be straight as a bird's beak," I told him.

"And the swelling has gone down considerably, Ethan," Ruth added.

A whistle came from the kitchen and Ruth hopped off the couch and disappeared through a doorway. When she returned she was cradling a mug with both hands.

"Some hot chocolate." She smiled as she placed the mug in front of Ethan. "A good warm cup of hot chocolate makes everything feel better."

I watched as Ruth gently placed her hand on Ethan's head and pushed his hair to the side like she would a schoolboy.

"I should press charges!" Ethan complained, with a hint of anger creeping into his voice for the first time since he was punched. "That thug needs to be in jail."

"Yes," I nodded. "You should talk to the police."

Ethan grew quiet again after my words.

"Why did he do that?" Ethan asked in a tone that sounded more hurt than angry.

"I think he said why," Ruth replied, handing Ethan a napkin. "You have some hot chocolate on your chin, Ethan."

Ethan quickly mopped up the stray droplets.

"Were you giving your brother needles and money for drugs?" I finally asked.

"It's not what it sounds like," Ethan mumbled.

"It's a simple question," I pressed.

"I didn't want him using dirty needles," Ethan quickly answered. "He might have gotten hepatitis or something worse if he used a dirty needle. I just wanted him to be safe."

"And the money?" I pressed. "Were you giving him money, too?"

"He was homeless…" Ethan whispered.

"Did you want him to stop using drugs?" Ruth asked. "Giving him needles and money weren't going to help him quit."

"I wanted him to stop," Ethan said, his voice breaking after his statement.

"But you gave him money *and* needles," I pointed out. "If you wanted him to stop…you wouldn't have been giving him anything."

"He was my brother," Ethan sighed. "He wasn't strong enough to just stop. My father thought he was but…I knew him better than dad. I just didn't want Joey to suffer."

"He had an addiction," Ruth pointed out. "He needed to suffer to break the addiction."

"You don't understand," Ethan said, and his voice grew softer by the end of the sentence.

"We had a plan."

"What?" Ruth asked.

"We…I mean…I…I thought we had a plan," Ethan softly spoke.

"What kind of plan?" I asked.

"A way for him to give up drugs without the pain of withdrawal," Ethan explained and he sat up on the couch and put the ice pack on the table.

"And how is that possible?" Ruth asked.

"I would give him money and he would buy fewer drugs each month," Ethan explained. "After every month I'd give him less money to get drugs. We thought…if he bought fewer drugs each month it would make it easier to break his habit. That was our plan."

"And did it work?" I asked.

"No," Ethan said, raising his voice. "It didn't work and it was all his fault!"

"Joseph?" Ruth asked.

"Yes!" Ethan said.

"What did Joseph do?" Ruth asked.

"He wanted more money," Ethan began. "He told me that much. Like I said, in the beginning we talked and agreed that it would be best if he eased his body off a little every month. That was the plan. Then he started asking for the same amount of money every month. I…I didn't understand why. Finally, I stood my ground. I told him I was giving him less money for the following month. I told him that was our plan. He didn't like that very much."

"What did he do?" I asked sitting on the couch next to Ethan. I could see his eyes begin to blink very quickly.

"It's just us here, Ethan," Ruth said. "No one else is listening but us."

Ethan sat with his hands on his lap. He was clearly afraid to say anymore and I wasn't quite sure if he would.

"You know Thomas has a picture of Joseph on his desk," I began. "Thomas says he looks at that picture and remembers better times with Joseph. I noticed that you don't have a picture of your brother on your desk, Ethan. Thomas didn't keep in touch with Joseph like you did. So why don't you have a picture of him in your office?"

Again, Ethan remained perfectly still on the couch, but Ruth and I could see his face growing red and his eyes filling with tears.

"We met one night in front of St. John's Church," Ethan finally spoke, barely louder than a whisper. The way he stared out at nothing in particular told me the memories were still fresh in his mind.

"And what happened that night?" I asked.

"I told him his plan wasn't working," Ethan recalled. "I told him he wasn't getting any better. Every time we spoke he needed more needles and more money. I finally couldn't keep up with it. I was sneaking out from work. I was keeping this from my family. I was just exhausted. So that night, in front of our church, I gave him a few dollars and clean needles and told him that was all I was giving him. I told him I was done with our plan."

"He must have been quite upset about that," Ruth observed.

Ethan nodded his head and wiped away some tears that began to roll down his cheeks.

"He yelled and complained that I was like dad," Ethan said in a quivering voice. "I told him I agreed to give him the needles under the condition that he wean himself off his addiction. I told him he was still spending the same amount of money and that nothing had changed. So I cut him off that night."

"Right there on the steps of our church," I guessed.

Ethan grew quiet and looked around at both of us. His eyes were red and his cheeks were becoming quite flushed.

"That's when he came at me," Ethan whispered.

"He came at you?" I asked, leaning forward in my seat. "What do you mean, Ethan?"

"He tackled me on the steps to the church," Ethan stated. "The way he hit me I lost my balance, spun around and landed on him. I don't know if it was the force of my body on top of his or if he was just falling fast, but the back of his head snapped back on the edge of those stone steps. I got up as fast as I could, but Joseph didn't. Then I looked down at him...and his eyes were wide open...and he wasn't breathing at all....and blood was everywhere."

Ethan started to cry and shake like a schoolboy does when he doesn't want to let his emotions come out in front of others.

"I called for help!" Ethan said, his voice going up. "I tried to get in the church but the doors were locked. I'd left my phone in my car and as I walked back to get it I started thinking about everything that was going to happen to me...how the police would question me...how my parents would be called in. How all of Washington would read about the Campbell family and how one son killed another. It wasn't just me...it was my whole family that would have been affected by the news. When I reached my car I couldn't bring myself to turn around and see my brother lying in a pool of blood. I was just afraid of what was going to happen to my family and me. So I got in the car and drove away that night."

Ethan paused and wiped away some more tears from his cheeks.

"I think about seeing Joseph on the steps every night," Ethan mumbled. "I haven't slept well since this happened. I...I just never thought he would die because he was angry with me. Brothers fight all the time, but they don't die because of it."

Ruth and I had nothing to say. What was there to say? One brother was going to carry the guilt of another brother's death with him forever. Mind you, he didn't kill Joseph. If you ask me, Joseph's addiction killed him that night.

CHAPTER TWENTY-FOUR: RESOLUTION

"So that's it?" Neil Cabbott asked without looking up from his notepad. He lowered his pen and tipped his head back and began to slowly bend it from side to side in an attempt to stretch his stiff neck. "It was the brother who murdered him?"

"I wouldn't say that," Charlotte sighed and she glanced over to Ruth.

"What would you call it?" Neil asked, rubbing his neck with one hand.

"A family tragedy if there ever was one," Charlotte replied.

"You know what it reminds me of, sister?" Ruth spoke up.

"What?" Charlotte asked.

"Lyndon Johnson," Ruth replied.

Charlotte laughed at the comment. It was such a strange connection Charlotte couldn't help but burst out in laughter. She could tell by the scowl on Ruth's face that she wasn't amused by the reaction.

"What on earth made you think of him, sister?" Charlotte finally asked.

"I can remember when Lyndon Johnson came to our church," Ruth recalled. "We were young women at the time, but I do remember that he was just this tall big man with this deep growling voice. I also remember how, before church started, he always got down on his knees and prayed before the service began. While most of us sat and let our minds wander while we waited for the service to begin, Johnson would always be in deep prayer. Do you recall that?"

"Vaguely," Charlotte replied.

"At the time, I thought President Johnson seemed like a good church-going man," Ruth continued. "When I look back now, I think he came to our church with a lot of conflict. I mean, there he was in our church, going through the motions of being a good Christian. Then he would return to the White House to meet with his generals about how best to bomb more people in Vietnam. As a Christian, I'm quite certain he began to serve as president with the best of intentions. However, like Ethan, sometimes the best of intentions can go wrong."

Neil looked at Ruth and nodded before putting his pen away. He remained silent and began to flip through the pages of notes he'd taken through the morning and afternoon.

"You two were very smart to figure all this out," he said, glancing up with a smile.

"I don't know about the word 'smart' but I would say we're very persistent about it," Ruth replied.

"Yes," Charlotte added. "Once we start something…we never give up."

"Well…thank you, ladies," he finally announced. "It's been a most interesting day. Now that I have what I need…I guess I'll make a few phone calls to the Campbell family members and get their reaction to the story I'm going to write."

"That would be a good place to start…if you had a family to call," Charlotte pointed out.

"What do you mean?" Neil asked.

"The Campbells are gone," Charlotte announced.

"Gone?" Neil asked. "What do you mean?"

"Miles retired last month," Charlotte began. "He and Natalie decided to move to the Caribbean. I forget which island, but I'm quite certain the warm trade winds agree with them in their retirement."

"Well, then...I'll call the Campbell children," Neil suggested.

"Didn't Thomas get another teaching job with a different college?" Ruth asked.

"Yes," Charlotte nodded. "He went somewhere out to the west coast. Seems the warm weather lured him away from Washington, too. I just hope he has a bigger office at his new college."

"Yes," Ruth agreed. "And Ethan went to England. Seems there was a gallery over there looking for a curator. Ethan thought a change of scenery would do him some good. Given what happened, I think that was a good idea."

"And Grace Campbell?" Ethan asked.

"She and her husband have also re-located," Charlotte grinned. "Young love can cause newlyweds to move. They thought living in the city wasn't the best place to raise a family. They now have acres of land...but I forget where that is."

Neil stood up with the kind of urgency that only a newspaper reporter would. His hands curled into fists, he reached for the ceiling and moaned while he stretched like the cat does after napping on our couch. He tipped his wrist to one side, glanced at his phone and his eyebrows shot up.

"I'll find them," Neil replied. "I'm a reporter and I'm pretty good at digging for information. I'll track them down. It'll just take a little longer to pull my story together."

"May I just say this," Charlotte stated, and she cleared her throat to make her voice clear as a bell. "A family is like an onion. When you first see a family, you're drawn to the outer layers—the clothes, the jewelry, and their general appearance. After a while, you peel away the outer layers and listen to their words, consider their thoughts and eventually work your way to the most important layer of any family…their heart. The Campbells are a good family. They have always loved one another and cared for each other. I believe that's the kind of insight your editor wanted me to give you about this family. I also believe that's why he discouraged you from writing this story."

"So what are you going to do with all of those notes?" Ruth asked.

"Write my story of course," he quickly said, tucking his notepad into this shirt. His eyes flicked down to the floor like he was addressing it instead of Ruth and Charlotte. "I mean it is my job. I should write about it…unless my editor shoots me down again."

Charlotte shook her head and turned to Ruth.

"Being responsible for your brother's death is enough of a burden," Ruth stated. "You don't need to write a story to add more weight to Ethan's burden."

"That's true, sister," Charlotte began. "When I think of Ethan's situation now I think of the words of Franklin Roosevelt. He said, "Men are not prisoners of fate, but only prisoners of their own minds." Ethan has to live with this terrible incident for the rest of his life. He loved his brother. He was aiding him in a misguided attempt to help Joseph overcome his addiction. He never intended his efforts to lead to his brother's death. That is a sad burden to carry through life."

"A brother who is a drug addict dying because he wrestles with another brother for drug money…it is a tragedy for everyone involved," Ruth observed.

"Agreed," Charlotte nodded, before turning her eyes to Mr. Cabbott.

"Well…thank you for your time today," he added before stepping out into the hallway and heading for the front door.

"We quite enjoyed meeting you," Ruth said.

"It looks like your cat wasn't impressed with me," he observed while pointing down to Mezzo, who was stretched out on the cool hardwood floor.

"She's a tough one to get any sign of affection from," Ruth explained.

Charlotte opened the door and led him outside. Glancing out to the street, Charlotte recognized the after-work traffic flowing by. The sun had arced behind some trees and the clouds in the sky were more golden than white. Charlotte and Ruth watched Mr. Cabbott descend from their porch, turn and offer a quick wave before opening the squeaky iron gate to leave the yard.

"Mr. Cabbott!" Charlotte called out.

"Yes," he answered, lingering by the gate.

Charlotte quickly descended down the steps from the front porch and met him at the gate.

"I know I've talked your ear off today, but since your editor sent you to us to "learn something" about Washington, let me give you one thought and then I promise not to speak again," Charlotte grinned.

The words caused Mr. Cabbott to turn and face Charlotte.

"Fancy a party," Charlotte began. "Fancy a party with beautiful people dressed in beautiful clothes sipping the best wine and indulging in the decadence of the finest hors d'oeuvres from the best chef in town. Imagine that if you will. Then, imagine how the guests move around the room. How they move and linger and move again. This is the dance that socialites know all too well. It's a carefully timed two-step that involves an exchange of pleasantries with one guest before moving on to the next guest."

"Why are you telling me this?" he sighed.

"When I attend such events," Charlotte continued, "I find my eyes aren't necessarily drawn to the people who move in this manner. My eyes are drawn to the people who are not moving. The quiet people who linger in the background or in the corners."

"You mean people who are just sitting around not talking?" he asked.

"Exactly," Charlotte smiled. "The ones who are blending in."

"It seems to me that if those people are by themselves it's because they are boring or don't have anything interesting to say," he observed.

"On the contrary," Charlotte replied. "Those are the most interesting people at the party. You see, they try to blend in because they know things they don't wish to talk about. That's why they simply choose not to indulge in the Socialite Two-Step. Those are the people I watch for.

Those are the people I find myself drawn to. Seeking out those kinds of people reveals more about them to me than a hundred frivolous conversations about the latest fashions or whose husband is rascaling around with what young thing."

"Again, why are you telling me this?" he sighed.

"Having your name plastered all over the front page of your paper with some sensational murder will make you well known to most readers," Charlotte nodded. "However, it will also drive away the more subtle readers who can be good sources for future stories. People like Ruth and myself."

"So what are you suggesting?" he asked, stepping closer to Charlotte.

"The Campbells are no longer in Washington, but there are people far more interesting to investigate around here," Charlotte grinned. "You seem to have more energy than Ruth and me put together. Let us help you with another story. A story that will justify pointing the finger at a person who is more evil than Ethan Campbell."

"A new story?" he asked.

"Look around your office and see if you can find another story that will interest you," Charlotte instructed. "When you find that story, and you are in need of some assistance, come around again and we will help you sort things out. We know every person and every secret in Washington, Mr. Cabbott. Take a pass on the Campbell family and come back again with a juicy story that you want to write about. We'll be here waiting for you."

Neil Cabbott showed no expression after these words. Instead, he simply turned and walked away. Charlotte and Ruth stood on the front step to their home watching him slip out the wrought iron gate that wrapped around their small yard. They watched him vanish into the bodies of other people who usually walked by their home in the evening.

"What do you think he'll do?" Ruth asked.

"I honestly don't know," Charlotte replied.

CHAPTER TWENTY-FIVE: TIME AND PATIENCE

In the days and weeks that followed, Charlotte and Ruth found their morning routine began to change in a good way. Where breakfast had once been a time to let their eyes scan articles for more clues into Joseph Campbell's death, they now found themselves skimming the headlines with less intensity. They also found themselves spending more time lingering over breakfast, occasionally having to heat up their oatmeal while they spoke about stories on politics, entertainment, or even advice columns.

As the days went by, they enjoyed the articles they found, but in the back of their minds they knew that Mr. Cabbott would eventually write something about Joseph Campbell's death. For a number of mornings, they cracked open the paper in anticipation of finding Mr. Cabbott's article. Both of them hoped they had talked some sense into Mr. Cabbott to persuade him not to write a story. Finally, one morning, Ruth could hear laughter coming from behind a section of the paper that Charlotte was holding.

"What's so funny, sister?" Ruth asked.

"I think Mr. Cabbott decided to take our advice," Charlotte stated and she pointed to one section of the paper that she was holding.

"What makes you says that?" Ruth asked, lowering her newspaper.

"Read this," Charlotte said, passing the paper over to Ruth.

"Lafayette Square Sisters Charm Reporter," Ruth read and she placed the article down on the kitchen table. "Oh my goodness. Don't tell me he made us the subject of his news story."

"I'm afraid so," Charlotte laughed. "It appears he wrote a lifestyle piece instead of a story about Joseph's death."

"Well, this is embarrassing," Ruth laughed. "At least he doesn't have our picture attached to the article."

"It does appear that he has our life story in there," Charlotte nodded while she closely examined the article. "Apparently he was listening more closely than either one of us thought."

"I wonder why he did this?" Ruth asked.

"I suspect he had a deadline to meet and he had to write something," Charlotte replied, shaking her head at the story.

"While I find this article rather embarrassing," Ruth said, folding up the paper, "'I'm happy he's kept the Campbell family out. I must say I've grown tired of spending my mornings lingering at this breakfast table, scanning the newspaper, searching articles that contain tidbits about Joseph's death. With summer time underway, I think we should be spending more of our mornings outside…not huddled over newspapers."

"Agreed," Charlotte said, squinting out the window to their small courtyard in the back of the house. "It does look like a nice day out there. However, before we talk about our plans for today, I was wondering if you saw the article about a fundraiser for Senator Robert Creed. Seems he wants to be president one day. Should we buy some tickets and hear him out?"

"Hmm," Ruth smiled. "A social event that doesn't involve snooping around for clues. I don't know, Charlotte, it will be awfully hard to go back to making frivolous chit-chat about things of little consequence."

"Remember," Charlotte advised. "It's the quiet people, the little things that tend to lead to the bigger, more interesting discoveries. I'm quite confident that the terribly dull Senator Creed may have a few interesting sides to him. We simply need to find them."

A few minutes later, breakfast was over and they began to clean up. With the sound of dirty dishes clanking in the kitchen, a loud knock on the front door caused Charlotte to step away from the sink and down the hallway. Ruth followed behind as Charlotte quickly closed her robe and tightened the sash around it.

"You open it," Charlotte said, moving down the hallway. "I look a mess."

"Nobody should be visiting this early," Ruth complained as she reached for the door knob. "Whoever is standing at this door is going to get a firm lecture from me on manners. Specifically, call before you visit!"

"Salesman," Charlotte mumbled. "I'll bet it's a salesman."

"So rude," Ruth mumbled back.

Ruth quickly jerked open the door with Charlotte staying off to the side so she wasn't in the sight line of whoever it was. When the door was opened, both sisters were relived to see Neil Cabbott, standing on their front porch. While he appeared with a smile on his face, the expression quickly changed when he saw that Ruth and Charlotte were still in their robes and slippers.

"I...I'm sorry," Neil said. "I've been working on this story and I needed some help. I guess I should have called first."

"Good manners would dictate such," Ruth mumbled.

"What are you writing about?" Charlotte asked, always the more curious of the two sisters.

Mr. Cabbott reached into his jacket pocket and pulled out his small spiral note pad from his vest pocket. Together Charlotte and Ruth stood on the porch with Neil Cabbott and listened to the latest mystery he had just uncovered in Washington.

Charlotte listened to him while she glanced beyond her front door step. The cars were driving by her house, as they often would most mornings. People also walked by, moving with the same kind of urgency with which the cars drove. Blue sky filled a gap between two tall buildings. A cardinal swooped down onto the top of their gate, head darting from side to side, then flew off again. Then she looked at her guest, who continued to speak.

"Mr. Cabbott," Charlotte began. "Come back in one hour…then we will help you."

"So you want me to stand out here?" he asked.

"Go for a walk," Charlotte suggested and she pointed to Lafayette Square in the distance. "Enjoy the lovely day before we help you with work."

As she watched him cross the street and head towards Lafayette Square Park, Charlotte noted again how the traffic moved in the street, how the people took quick strides to get to their destination, and how the cardinal was now a dot in the sky flying into a deep crest of blue.

Charlotte turned to Ruth and smiled.

"Things are in motion this morning," Charlotte observed, glancing across the street at the people cutting through Lafayette Square. "It's another morning for important people to spin around this city with great urgency. I like having a good mystery to make me feel that way, too."

Yes, things are in motion, sister. It's another day and things are in motion."

To most passersby, two old ladies closing the front door of their home might lead one to conclude that these were two sisters about to lead another quiet day of solitude and reflection on a life well led. However, like most of the commuters walking about this morning, the Dupree sisters also had a sense of urgency to their morning.

CHAPTER TWENTY-SIX: EPIPHANY AT THE PARK

Later in the afternoon, after they had answered many questions for Mr. Cabbott, Charlotte took a stroll to Lafayette Square. Walking under another pristine blue sky, she reflected on her meeting with Mr. Cabbott earlier in the morning. She also thought back on the events of the last few weeks. The difficulties in unraveling the secrets to Joseph Campbell's death were still fresh in her mind.

While she walked through the park, Charlotte could sense that summer was beginning to fade into the embrace of autumn. The sun was a bit lower in the sky. The air was more dry than humid. The shadows were growing longer by the day. Even a few people walking by Charlotte were beginning to wear long sleeves rather than t-shirts.

When she arrived at the entrance to the park, Charlotte folded her hands in front of her waist, turned and simply looked at the traffic filling both sides of the street. She watched the occasional cab whiz by, as if expecting one of them to stop for her. Suddenly she saw a long black limo slow down and pull up to the curb where she was standing. The window lowered and Charlotte quickly recognized the face. It was the reason she'd come to Lafayette Square. She'd come to meet Lucille Vance.

"Hello, Lucille," Charlotte smiled.

"I told the driver to wait here while we speak," Lucille explained. "Whatever you want to talk about, make it brief. I have another engagement to get to today and I don't want to be late."

"Why not step out and stand here with me?" Charlotte asked. "It's a beautiful day."

"I'm fine right here," Lucille quickly replied. "Now you asked me to meet you here and I was able to work you into my schedule. So what is this pressing matter that you wanted to share with me? Is it about that Joseph Campbell matter?"

"It is," Charlotte replied, leaning her head down to the open window. "The last time we spoke, I thought you promised to call me with more information about his death. As the days went by, I thought it odd that you never got back to me."

"I was busy," Lucille sighed. "Sometimes I'm too busy to remember my promises."

"We both know every discreet fact in this town finds its way back to you," Charlotte continued. "What happened to Joseph...well...you never called with the rest of the story, which I found very curious. I know you, Lucille. You have many resources to draw from to fill in the blanks about something, which is why I expected to hear from you. Then I remembered something."

"And what was that, Charlotte?" Lucille asked with a curious grin on her ruby red lips.

"You're the godmother to Ethan Campbell," Charlotte stated. She paused for a moment and watched Lucille's eyes glance down to her purse. "I never thought you were one to respect discretion, Lucille, but then I realized you already knew what Ethan did. You knew it from the time Ruth and I walked into your house. You led us to believe you were as much in the dark as we were about Joseph's death."

"Really, Charlotte?" Lucille sighed. "You know I'm never in the dark."

"Well, we both know how sensitive Ethan is," Charlotte continued. "When that accident happened with Joseph, he must have been so distraught. It must have been tearing him apart knowing he couldn't say anything to his family. I know it was traumatic for Ethan, and he had to tell someone. Other than his parents and siblings, you're the closest thing to family Ethan has. You see, Ethan and I would speak at church, Lucille. He told me how you were there when he graduated from college. He told me how you were there to support him when he first thought about managing an art gallery. I've been close to the Campbell family for many years. I know how close you are to Miles and Natalie. I remember how slighted I felt when Natalie asked you to hold baby Ethan for his baptism instead of me."

"A bitter pill to swallow?" Lucille grinned while glancing at her watch.

"Your driver doesn't have enough gas for us to have that conversation," Charlotte observed. "No matter...from what Ethan has told me you've been a good godmother over the years. I just didn't think you were capable of keeping what he did to Joseph a secret."

Lucille looked up and smiled. It was the kind of smile she used when people were surprised by a revelation or rumor she was passing along to them. It was a satisfying expression that reminded Charlotte of a cat that had successfully cornered a mouse and was about to devour it. If Lucille had a tail, Charlotte thought, it would be wagging.

"Oh, Charlotte," Lucille smiled. "You were always too smart for your own good. Now you must excuse me, I'm running late."

With that, the window to the cab went up and the limo slowly pulled away. Charlotte watched Lucille's limo merge with other traffic and disappear into the bustle of the city. Charlotte merely sighed and began to walk through the entrance to Lafayette Square to think about what had just happened.

Sitting on a park bench, reflecting on her revelation, Charlotte was lost in her thoughts. She had the vague sense that the park was filled with activity. It was a sense that she didn't care to confirm by standing up and walking around to investigate the details. Instead, she was too occupied with her thoughts to care. All she could think about was how Lucille had managed to keep the secret that Ethan killed his brother. It was the kind of loyalty that not too many godmothers would show to their godchild.

After a few minutes, Charlotte looked around at some joggers go by. Then she spotted Ruth walking briskly through the park entrance and down the sidewalk. Her head turned from side to side until she spotted Charlotte sitting on the bench.

"You left," Ruth said.

"I had some thinking to do," Charlotte replied. "Are you done weeding your garden?"

"Yes," Ruth replied, brushing her hands together in a half-hearted attempt to knock more loose dirt from her fingers. "Why did you leave without telling me, sister? I didn't know where you went until I saw your note on the kitchen table. How dare you take a walk in the park without me? You know I do so enjoy taking walks with you."

"Well, it wasn't just a walk. You see, Ruth, I had a brief meeting with Lucille Vance," Charlotte explained. "I got the sense that you'd had your fill of Lucille after our last visit with her. That's why I didn't tell you."

Ruth made a face and the expression told Charlotte that her suspicions were correct.

"Why did you want to see her again?" Ruth asked.

"Because I had to confirm a long held suspicion that Lucille knew about Joseph's accidental death," Charlotte stated.

"What made you think that?" Ruth asked.

"Did you forget that she is Ethan's godmother?" Charlotte asked.

"Oh," Ruth answered and then she smirked. "As if that poor boy doesn't have enough problems."

"When I remembered that, it got me thinking about Ethan's situation," Charlotte nodded. "I'm certain he was quite upset about what happened. Since he couldn't tell his parents, Lucille was more than willing to lend Ethan a sympathetic ear to listen to his...problem."

"Of course," Ruth laughed. "She'll use anyone to grab some gossip."

"That's the interesting part," Charlotte said, pointing at Ruth. "Even though she learned Ethan's secret...she guarded it. I don't think she told a soul what happened."

"She what?" Ruth asked.

"She kept a secret and I think she did it out of love," Charlotte stated. "I know you don't think the best of Lucille, but as much as you might not want to hear this, I believe this reveals a side of Lucille that you doubt existed. It would appear that, underneath all of her coy grins and poisonous rumors, she does indeed have a heart."

"The only way she'd have a heart is if she ate one," Ruth giggled.

"Really, sister!" Charlotte snapped. "That's not a very nice thing to say about someone we've both known for a number of years. Besides, she loved Ethan enough to keep his secret. That tells me what kind of godmother she is. One that stands by her godson no matter what."

Suddenly, a loud sound surged from above. Charlotte and Ruth both looked up, expecting to see a dark rain cloud overhead. Instead, they saw the president's helicopter, Marine One, shooting across the sky towards the White House to either pick up or drop off the Commander in Chief.

For Charlotte it was a reminder of how easy it was to get lost in the big broad strokes of Washington D.C. How easily one can get swept up in the politics, the power, the buildings, and the symbols of the city. Even the occasional limousines that cut through the streets could pique one's curiosity with their tinted windows. For Ruth and Charlotte, the newspaper they looked at each morning could set their tone for the day with one headline. They were the kinds of distractions that always caught Charlotte's eye and kept her mind engaged. Up until a few weeks ago, it was always the broad strokes that interested her.

When Joseph Campbell's story came along, it was such a small story it barely caught her eye. Yet, from such a small detail came a bounty of revelations. The death of a homeless man, the secrets of a prominent family, and a resolution that she could have never imagine changed the way Charlotte now saw her city.

From this experience, she found herself more attuned to the smaller things around her. She would be less distracted by the larger headlines she read every morning. Instead, she would try to focus on the smaller stories and the lesser curiosities that Washington presented to her. She would focus more on the smaller details of a city filled with broad strokes.

THE END

ABOUT THE AUTHOR

Allen B. Boyer is the author of two Young Adult novels and one nonfiction book about the West Point Academy and its famous graduates. His books have been sold around the country. His Bess Bullock Retirement Home Mystery series produced five mysteries for Cozy Cat Press. *Death at the Presidents Church* begins his new Dupree Sisters Mystery series.

Mr. Boyer lives near Hershey, Pennsylvania, with his wife, Suzanne, and their three children. He likes to take his children and their dog to visit residents at a nearby retirement home.

www.ingramcontent.com/pod-product-compliance
Lightning Source LLC
Chambersburg PA
CBHW020332260626
47156CB00004B/1483